INCENDIARY

Incendiary
Edited by Weasel

ISBN-13: 978-1-948712-81-1

Copyright © 2021 Izzy T. AKA Weasel
Cover image from http://www.goonwrite.com/

Printed in the U.S.A.

Sinister Stoat Press
an imprint of Weasel Press
Lansing, MI
http://www.weaselpress.com/sinister-stoat

CONTENTS

Most editors write these long introductions to anthologies. Honestly, I keep these short. As a reader you don't need an extra five pages explaining what you're holding. You have a good idea as it is. But we're here. 2020 is over and 2021 is just starting out. There has been so much rage felt within these past several months. And containing that anger is a daunting chore. Incendiary is an anthology that examines that anger. In some cases, it might not be the worst factor here. In this book you may encounter cases of Violence, Murder, Transphobia, homophobia, sexism, sexual assault, fat shaming, racism, domestic violence, and abusive relationships. Although this is a horror anthology, I won't tell you to keep the lights on. But I will tell you to tread lightly.

Izzy T. AKA Weasel
The Dude
Sinister Stoat Press

INCENDIARY

EDITED BY
WEASEL

Sinister Stoat Press

PARK BENCH
WILLOW ALVAREZ

"I thought you had a heart, but instead you have a spade. Don't you?" I spoke the words quickly. They tickled my tongue. Made it feel hairy.

"What the fuck does that even mean?" He frowned awkwardly and shifted his weight side to side. He couldn't look me in the eye. "It's just I found someone else. It's nothing against you. I don't get why you're being so hard about this."

"I mean spades look just like hearts," I paused for effect. I wanted to see if he'd make eye contact. He didn't. "I thought you had a heart, but you just have a tool for digging. I guess you didn't find what you were looking for."

He stopped frowning at that. His face was carefully blank. He looked around at the park. I'm guessing to see if anyone was nearby. It was late. I'd invited him out. He wasn't answering my texts or calls. So I left him a note under his apartment door. A time, a place, scribbled hastily between dried tears. "I don't know what you want from this. I was pretty clear."

"Not talking to me isn't clear. Josh," I huffed. His name was foreign now. Like a curse word you extract from a frazzled foreigner. You know its nature. But you can't quite understand its meaning. You know you got it from pressure. It's not something freely given. "Can we sit down?"

He motioned to a park bench. I thought I couldn't cry anymore, but that turned out to be wrong. Tears trickled down my already puffy face, but I still smiled and nodded at his tacit approval of sitting. I followed him and we sat a respectful two hand distance from each other. Not quite at the end of the bench, but we could both touch the cold arm rest, and even lean on it if we felt the need.

"I'm being clear now. We're done. I found someone else. She wouldn't be happy to know I was with my ex-girlfriend in the middle of a park at 1fucking AM. Fuck. Sammy. Why so late?" He looked exasperated. Maybe ashamed? I wasn't sure if it was shame for how he treated me, or being with me? Maybe both? It hurt.

"Fuck you Josh," I spat looking up at the stars. I saw the big dipper. I wondered if it could pick me up and take me from here. Or pick him up and drop him in a lake.

"Fine I'-"

I cut him off before he could get up to leave, "I knew you wouldn't meet me during the day."

That seemed to strike a chord because he relaxed. I didn't have to look at him to tell. I could feel it in the way the cicadas droning seemed less ominous. Less like a death dirge. Now it was more like a prelude. I couldn't tell to what.

"Fine talk. Say what you need to say. Then we can go our separate ways. No communication. She's the one Sammy. I'm not fucking it up." He sounded unabashedly happy then. It was a cruel sort of happiness. Like when one child steals another toy. Happiness from pain, or perhaps in spite of someone else's. I felt the tree limbs reach out for me too. After he spoke the words, an elder tree's branches creaked loudly. I knew what it wanted. I couldn't give it to them yet.

"She cis?" I asked quickly. My voice strained from keeping the more active tree at bay. I could feel the ants start to scurry closer too. Even the bushes on either side of the bench started to send creeping vines in the night towards the bench. I kept them at bay. I couldn't let them. I hoped he thought the strain in my voice was from the situation, not my subconscious reaction to it. He never really believed in magic anyway.

He scoffed after a few seconds, "You really want to know?"

I turned to face him and finally he looked at me. He didn't seem sad. Or even the least bit regretful. "Yes." I whispered back. My voice almost like a snake.

"Of course she fucking is. Sammy. I wasn't going to stay with a tranny. You knew that. I tol—" one of the elder tree's branches snapped startling him to stand, "what the fuck."

I didn't get up or move. I just watched him look around. Trying to peer through the darkness to see what was lurking in the shadows. I choose this park because it was notoriously unlit, and illegal to be in after dark. Though it was also well known that the police never actually enforced that law. I'd come here with Josh many times before. Around this same spot.

"I think I should go," he put his hands in his coat pockets and turned to leave.

"Wait," I said the words and he did. My voice was soaked in glamour. It sounded like echos and honey and wasps flying. He couldn't move. "Sit with me."

He turned back towards me. His movements were jagged. Obviously forced. I'd never done this before. At least not in this context. I'd used glamour here or there to get out of a bill or something like that, but I'd never actually commanded someone. I felt a rush. I turned to face him and he looked terrified.

If I was honest, he wasn't all that handsome. I mean, I was objectively more attractive. But I was also 6ft and had broad shoulders. So, whether or not I looked like a model was irrelevant in a small Midwestern town where everyone knew you were a freak to begin with. Being statuesque just made you stand out. Made my dysphoria translate that word into manly.

"What did you do to me? Did you use some of your weird Caribbean voodoo powder or some shit?" His voice sounded surer than I would have expected. False bravado? He was good at pretending. I ignored all the tarot readings saying that he didn't love me. I really believed he cared.

"I didn't drug you Josh," my voice was normal again, though somewhat deflated. I couldn't look up at him so I looked at the elder tree which slowly brought it's limbs closer and closer. Josh must have followed my line of vision because he gasped.

"You always said they waved, not that you could fucking control them!" His voice was more frantic now. Anxious. "What the fuck are you?"

"Was any of it real? Did you ever really care about me?" He didn't respond so I turned to look at him. His eyes were closer together than I would have liked, and his nose was bulbous. He looked somewhat like a pig. I was surprised I'd just noticed that. Had he always looked so piglike? "Be honest with me." The glamour was back and Josh's face turned pale. He opened his mouth to speak, then closed it, then opened it again.

Finally, the words came out in a typhoon, "I thought you were hot. Are hot. Your tits are huge and amazing, and somehow natural. And your skin is soft and clear. You made the best noises when I kissed you and you made me feel like a man. But I never loved you. I could never love something I couldn't take outside with me. Or couldn't bring home. You were something for me to have fun with before settling down. A secret addiction. I liked you well enough, but I never loved you."

I regarded him silently and he seemed to squirm under my gaze. He looked horrified at what he said. Maybe he wasn't even aware of all of it until he said it out loud. The tears kept falling from my eyes and made tributaries on my cheeks and splashes on the pavement. My heart felt like it had been rubbed raw with sandpaper.

"Do you love her?" I didn't know why I asked. I needed to know. I hadn't asked the twenty other times something like this happened to me. But we'd been together for a year and a half. I needed to hear him say it. My voice was still glamoured, but I honestly don't think it had to be. He spoke quickly enough.

"I think so. I'm happy with her at least. She's not as hot as you, but we fit."

I leaned back on the bench. Long curly black hair fell behind it. I stared at the stars and found Ursa Major. I felt all of the anger in my stomach, then my throat, then my tongue, then my lips, "choke on it then."

After the words left my mouth I felt the vessels of blood in his lungs break. He lunged forward holding his chest and began to heave phlegm and blood. Maybe he was trying to speak, I wasn't sure. I stared at the stars. And when his body was still I stared down at him in the fetal position. Saw the blood drain towards the roots of hungry plants. The ants coming to feat on his flesh. Got up. And walked away.

COME QUIETLY
LEAH BOND

Tara always had been an auditory creature. She knew there would be consequences to her and Jay's fascination with Kaiju porn. It took a month of frustration to realize she could only climax to the sound of screams.

Once this distinction had been discovered, Jay seemed eager to comply.

Despite the secluded suburban area in which they lived, noise complaints trickled into the police department. Search warrants. Alarmed neighbors. Those searches turned up little but torn posters of movie monsters and a pile of VHS tapes within their home.

Tara knew she was the impetus. Jay went to desperate lengths to chase her satisfaction.

Breaking into Patriot Park the night prior had been his idea. The empty coaster cars rattled above, a test run to their first drop. She could barely discern the murmur of potential riders as the park began to fill. Tara ducked into the shade within their hunting blind and shook her head; this development in their union left her to wonder if Jay hadn't become too eager to please.

That camouflaged blind was a yard sale find. Jay noticed it as the aging couple began to pack up at the end of the day and snagged it from their Free pile. She remembered how happy he was. He didn't hunt often, but when he did, he became absolutely consumed by the act.

Tara curled back onto the sleeping bag next to Jay. She watched him pretend to sleep, but his sudden smirk uncovered the ruse. Their lips met as the thunderous coaster raged overhead. The ride's next several rounds offered thrills and satisfaction for all.

The National Anthem could be heard in the distance as the animal mascots for which the park was famed held their daily March of Patriots.

Spent, Jay pulled Tara against his bulky chest as he leaned against one of the coaster's many support pillars. She stuffed the dismantled blind into his pack and withdrew a granola bar to share. They took turns munching mouthfuls of the honeyed oat brick.

Jay signaled for Tara to stop chewing so he could hear.

The March of Patriots had ended. Rollercoaster operations would soon resume. However, someone had wandered into the area.

They approached with purpose. A park employee?

Jay crouched behind the nearest pillar. Tara dashed across to conceal herself behind its neighbor.

The rhythmic crunch of dead foliage and fallen branches continued its progress through neglected underbrush. It headed straight to the spot where the blind had been, flattened and clear of debris. Jay signaled for Tara to meet the intruder.

Despite the increased shaking of her panicked palms, Jay whispered to her: "Pretend you're lost."

Her lips spread into a meek smile as she emerged.

Before her stood a park employee dressed in a Major Nutter squirrel costume, complete with gigantic cheeks and brown, fluffy oversized tail. Major Nutter paused in what she could only interpret as shock. Twenty feet separated them.

"Hey, I wandered off from my friends to explore and got sidetracked." She ended her statement with a nervous laugh, leaned to the side, one toe ground into the soil as she rocked that heel back and forth from her ankle and offered a shy grin.

"You're not supposed to be in this area," said the giant squirrel. Good. It was a higher pitch, maybe a woman or young man with a slight build. Major Nutter began to approach Tara.

"I couldn't help it. I can just be on my way..." Tara stepped backwards as she tried to distance herself from the squirrel. The brown mass of fur passed the pylon where Jay had hidden; he began to creep up behind Major Nutter.

"Better hurry. My boss is on his way, he'll make me take you in for processing." The squirrel's advance resumed.

Tara nodded, and continued to back away, wide-eyed. She looked at Jay and gasped. Major Nutter must have seen her eyes and expression shift, as the squirrel turned right into Jay's sucker punch. Major Nutter's exaggerated left cheek collapsed, followed by the rest of Major Nutter.

"Why'd you hit him, Jay? Now he's hurt! He would have let me go!"

"You heard him say processing," Jay knelt and removed Major Nutter's disfigured helmet."You know you'd be arrested, and we can't have that. Ooh! Look at all that acne." A pasty, pimpled young man with a two-guard buzz cut lay at their feet.

"And this isn't worse?" Tara asked in shock as Jay popped out the sunken cheek of the oversized squirrel head.

He handed it to her and said, "Put this on. I'll keep things under control, baby."

Jay unzipped the back of the suit, peeled the costume from the unconscious young man, and rummaged through its formless pockets.

"There it is!" Jay fumbled with a walkie talkie, and turned it off. He slid it underneath some bushes. "Put this on, too. We're walking out of here the way we came in. Don't talk to anyone. We belong here."

"Jay, I don't like this..."

"Just put on the suit, please. If you don't, I will."

"Ew! It smells like ...teenager." Tara stepped into the oversized legs of her new squirrel uniform. It sagged. Jay tightened the snaps and ran the zipper up her back to seal her inside.

"There. If anyone gives us any shit, flip them off and walk away. We get back to your truck, and head home. If the finger doesn't work, tell them you quit and storm off. Get back to your truck. Can you do that?" He slipped the helmet over her head and bent towards her to give her a questioning look.

"It really stinks in here."

"The sooner we get out of here, the sooner that helmet is gone. Got it?"

"Yeah."

Jay hoisted the pack and began the hike back to Tara's truck. She followed, but it was hard to see through the gauze inside Nutter's mouth, which served as a breathing area and provided sight.

"Slow down, would you? It's hard to see through this netting."

"You know we have to hurry."

They made it past the rollercoaster, and back through the

Alamo-themed section of the park, the way they had come.

"MOMMY!" a small voice squealed, "It's Major Nutter!! Take my picture with him!" Tara felt a pair of arms shackle her knees . They almost knocked her off balance.

"You're my favorite Servin' Critter! I love it when you steal all the rations and it's always you 'cept that one time Madge Badger did it..."

"Jay..." Tara called for Jay, who strolled across the walkway to vanish behind a hedge wall. She posed for a picture with the little boy and waved goodbye, only to turn and walk headfirst into an employee dressed as the infamous Madge Badger.

"You're not supposed to be here, boy. Get back to Freedom Feastin'," Madge's voice barked, deep and threatening.

She shook her head and continued on the path Jay had gone.

"Management will have your ass for this!!" the badger exclaimed. Tara turned and gave Madge the bird, which drew an angry reaction from some parents and their brood. A little girl jumped to Nutter's defense and started to hammer the back of Madge's thighs with her diminutive fists. "Why did you steal Major's rations this time?" Of course, like starved piranhas who caught their first scent of blood, Tara saw two, three, now ten children run to the scene. They began to scream, kick, hit, and um, badger... Madge. Parents began to yell, tried to restrain, but the frenzy had begun.

Tara waved farewell once more, wound her way around the hedge and into the brush. She could barely distinguish where Jay must have wandered. Onward she pressed. Where had he gone? Was this even the right path?

Relieved, she located the opening that Jay had lopped from the fence late the night before.

"Oh Major Nutter," she confessed, "I loved your show when I was a kid, but I'm glad to be out of you!"

Tara placed the hat next to the fence's cleft and unzipped her squirrel suit, which had become hot and sticky from her sweat. The zipper split, and she was able to work her body out of the gap, but the majority of the suit hung from the collar clamped around her neck.

"There you are!" Jay returned from beyond the fence to assist her.

"It's about time, jerk. Leaving me behind like that. Help me get out of this."

He brandished his pocketknife. "Hold still." Jay cut the suit away, and left her with a noose of brown fur. "There we go, doll. Perfect." He tugged her new collar. "Let's get."

"But my neck, this mess...hold on!" Tara jogged after Jay as he lugged the hollow, misshapen squirrel head. They ran to her truck in an empty corner of the massive parking lot.

"I wish you hadn't hit that guy." Tara said as the Chevy's engine sputtered to life. "We could have just snuck out, I'm sure."

"You know what he saw?"

"What did he see, Jay?"

"He saw you. You know what he didn't see?"

"Your fist."

"My face. If he remembers anything, it's you. You're the one that got us into this."

"Me? You're the one that planned all of this."

"And I did this all for you!" Jay spat. "Just get us home."

Tara drove home, her mood soured by Jay's sudden change in attitude.

Tara felt her personal liberties wither. Once she stepped through their front door, Jay's obsession with her increased; invitations declined, any suggestion she made that this became too much was dismissed. They talked this through-he had a vasectomy a while back, had he changed his mind?

Here the script inexplicably flipped and she became the troubled one, Jay devastated by her empty accusations. He risked everything for her, and to be left unappreciated, unacknowledged, unrewarded? Each confrontation moved the prong securing that leash one hole tighter-soon she would have no room to breathe.

In her frustrations, she held some freedom. During more pleasant sessions of their lovemaking, Tara would imagine herself the gigantic titan, crashing through skyscrapers, I-beams threaded through her teeth as destruction of cities entire fell to the rhythms of her crimson rush; invocations in scarlet rippled from the earth below, panicked cries risen in chant to the pulse of her racing heart. The mirage would soon fade as Jay pulled her close, his scent changed somehow, a once familiar accent become intimate invasion.

Their outing to Patriot Park soon became a sentence-long blip on the evening news, transformed into a memory of which they never spoke. Patterns resumed.

Tara felt her personal liberties wither. Once she stepped through their front door, Jay's obsession with her increased; invitations declined, any suggestion she made that this became too much was dismissed. They talked this through-he had a vasectomy a while back, had he changed his mind?

Here the script inexplicably flipped and she became the troubled one, Jay devastated by her empty accusations. He risked everything for her, and to be left unappreciated, unacknowledged, unrewarded? Each confrontation moved the prong securing that leash one hole tighter-soon she would have no room to breathe.

In her frustrations, she held some freedom. During more pleasant sessions of their lovemaking, Tara would imagine herself the gigantic titan, crashing through skyscrapers, I-beams threaded through her teeth as destruction of cities entire fell to the rhythms of her crimson rush; invocations in scarlet rippled from the earth below, panicked cries risen in chant to the pulse of her racing heart. The mirage would soon fade as Jay pulled her close, his scent changed somehow, a once familiar accent become intimate invasion.

Their outing to Patriot Park soon became a sentence-long blip on the evening news, transformed into a memory of which they never spoke. Patterns resumed.

"Tara, it's Kev – Got a showing up at the Litz Gallery off 8th this Friday, I'll be in town. Sorryfor the short notice, but I owe it all to Marty! He bought me plane tickets and a ho-tel room for a quick trip. I'd love to see-" There was a brief scramble of words as the message was deleted. Jay reset the answering machine and reached into the fridge to retrieve another beer. He sat at the dining room table and studied upcoming events in the current Weekly rag.

"Who was it?" Tara shouted down from the bathroom above.

"Just another magazine scammer," Jay flipped through the paper to the art section, and tore out the page which outlined Kev's event. He folded and then shoved it into his back pocket and asked, "Remember the one downtown you worked at? You won a cruise?"

"Ugh! Another freakin' boiler room." Tara shut the bathroom door.

Friday arrived without fanfare. Tara folded their laundry, bits of paper scattered among clothes in the dryer. She unfolded remnants of the ad for her friend Kev's exhibit, which had just ended. Clothes stacked, she placed the ad on top and carried them up to their bed, up to Jay.

"What the hell?"

"You know how I feel about 'Kev.'"

"Really? How do you feel about Kevin, Jay? We know it's

not jealousy, don't go there..."

"I just don't feel like sitting in a corner at some event I don't care about with people I don't know. There are better things we can do with our time."

"Kevin is my *friend*. I don't want to hang out with your friends all the time but I know you want me there, so I go. I don't get you sometimes, Jay."

"Whatever." He continued flipping channels, unfazed.

Tara stormed down the stairs to sulk on the couch. She returned to retrieve a blanket from their bed and retreated into a bottle of wine for the evening.

The next day, she came home from a trip to the office before Jay got back from a freelance gig. The machine was full of messages, and of course the first one was from Kev, disappointed that she couldn't make it to his showing, did she not get his first message? She jotted down the number he left and called him. The other calls were for Jay. Tara deleted them. She knew it was petty, but he did the same to her. Didn't even listen, just delete, delete, delete. His deletion was deliberate. Fuck him, she could do it, too. At least the sex was still good, and hopefully these potholes would pass. They had been good together so far, and she told herself this was just a rough patch, all relationships had them once in a while.

Kev chose Chubby's off 39th and Bordnell to meet for a meal that evening, an old haunt they once adored. Greasy as always, salty, cheese-covered shoestring fries with burgers so oily and thin, you weren't done until the grease dripped from at least one elbow. They always put one lone leaf of curly lettuce atop those caramelized onions to provide the illusion that it might be a little bit healthy. The pair finished their jovial feast of good memories with a towering milkshake and straws that were too long, almost losing a lung to vacuum up the nearly solid cream-topped fudgy sludge contained within. How many late nights were spent huddled in a corner booth, tears of heartbreak from a spurned lover, soul-shattering disapproval of Kev's parents resistant to his lifestyle, baring their true selves to one another without judgment, expectation, or shame?

Kev had Marty now, and for once, he was happy, truly happy. She had Jay. Was she? Her hesitation said plenty. They loitered in the parking lot for a good fifteen minutes afterward, noted upgrades to the old neighborhood, exchanged hugs and giggles before they returned to their separate vehicles, their separate lives. Neither noticed Jay's Volvo as it crept a distance behind Kev's rental, regimented, methodical. Tara returned to an unlit, vacant home. By the time Jay crawled in bed beside her, she had fallen fast asleep.

Burly Jay accosted Kev from behind as he returned to his room from the hotel parking lot. Jay put him in a sleeper hold. Easy. Once Kev had fallen unconscious, Jay baled him up with electrical tape and hefted Kevin's limp, wispy form into the trunk of his car. Jay drove to a rural, abandoned farmhouse and bound Kev to a workbench with a rope of coarse hemp.

He reinforced the gag, applied more tape around Kev's head, double checked the security of his restraints, then Jay returned home, to leave Kev overnight in the shadowed, frigid stillness.

Jay wanted to learn to drive a stick. Tara was happy to teach him. He would drive her truck when she was with him on the weekends, when they were together.

Tara asked, "Where are we off to today?"

"You'll see. It's a surprise." He cinched her blindfold of emerald felt and guided her into the truck. A guarding hand cupped the top of her head. He strapped her in, and swung the passenger door shut. The engine belched, turned over, and they scuttled into motion. The aging Chevy's clutch ground disapproval as he shifted too fast for its desire. Upshift lurches became ritual; the jolt and rattle from its worn shocks were a blinking sign that read *Slow Down.*

She felt him turn onto a gravel road. The crisp air, grate of tires tossing pebbles that pinged the undercarriage beneath her feet; feet that should have ran while grass still grew to grasp between her toes. That time had passed and all was grey and cold, parched with winter's chill, the streets here paved with etched frost of promises broken. Another gear rasped in anger.

"I know you're still learning, but please don't be so rough on my truck."

"I'll be as rough as I please."

His palm slid onto her thigh, gave it a firm squeeze of pain and lingered, torpid. The truck stopped moving. They both settled, silent as the dust behind them.

Everything about Jay felt different, off. Wrong. He led her into an empty farmhouse? A barn? He was more angry and loutish compared to past outings. He left her blindfolded, marched her along. He strapped her into place on an old bed in the middle of the room. She could hear him as he stepped around the bed to secure her, doubly so. Her wrists began to ache. Her hands started to tingle, binds were too tight.

"Wrists are too tight. My hands are going numb."

"Be a good girl and I might fix it."

Tara coughed from dust that Jay's efforts had shaken from the old headboard. He continued to initiate events despite her request to loosen those cords. Her blindfold started to slip from one side. A strap tickled her nose as it drooped. She felt the glittery tingle of a sneeze coming on as it built in her sinuses, from the bridge of her nose to the back of her throat. Jay leaned in for a kiss and she violently sneezed in response.

Her head came forward in reflex to bash against his cheek, along the side of his nose. His face dripped down with a few strings of her phlegm. Jay pulled the blindfold from her face to clean his own, now flushed with excitement, rage, or both. She could discern the difference no longer. *Had there ever been one?*

He stepped away from the bed to growl down at her, "Hold on while I get this fucking party started!" Blood trickled down his nostril, chased the edge of his lip, and traced a line to frame the jaw of this heartless man of tin made flesh.

He stomped into an adjacent room where muffled mumbles escaped to tell Tara that they were not alone. A much louder thump, then a gunshot (*oh god ohmygod what has he done*) came from the other room, followed by screams, many of them now her own. He returned to attempt a repeat of the amusement park, to lean in and kiss her, now a mimicked, mock affection that she no longer held any desire to fulfill. Tara turned her head to avoid his kisses and struggled against her binds all the more.

"Moonrocks! I never wanted you to hurt anyone, Jay"

"I'm doing this for you."

"You've been scaring me for a while, Jay, Moonrocks..."

Jay leaned in to initiate as she continued to struggle against her restraints; the dried, aged wood groaned, started to creak in protest to this repeated strain.

"Tara, I have done everything, yet you still fucking hurt me in return."

"I saw the red lights, thought this was a phase we'd get through. Moonrocks, Moonrocks! I'm done!"

"This the reward I get for the years we've had? Don't I get some consolation prize here, the least you could do is say *Yes Jay, I love you Jay*," he mocked, "like you do, but do you really?"

"Jay, I am serious as shit. Moonrocks!"

"That's rich," He laughed. "To think your little safeword will stop anything."

Kev woke to the pair's arrival. His muffled cries were not met with a response. As he continued to struggle against those restraints, one hand was almost free.

Jay stomped into the darkened room and hoisted his shotgun from where it rested against the wall. He thrust the butt end at Kev's head. Kev elicited a muffled scream. The impact knocked his gag loose. Jay turned the shotgun around and fired at the wall behind Kev in warning, which dislodged more dust and a few boards through the wall, admitting sunlight. Kev began to scream. Jay leaned the rifle against the wall and left.

Kev continued to work one hand free, then the other. He untied his legs. While Jay occupied himself screaming at Tara, Kev took the 12-guage and made sure another round was loaded in the chamber. He began to approach the bed Tara was tied to and slowly trained the gun at Jay. From his angle, the barrel rested directly above Tara's head.

Thunder pealed from above. Everything became mute, penetrating molasses. Its darkness bubbled up to pull her down, away from madness, down to the moon. *We live here now, live in the rocks.* Winter passed without fanfare; all became fluorescent sanitizer, her rise to the surface became eventual. A squirrel's throat pulsed in what would have been chatter, but remained suppressed by the insulated window. Kev's hand gripped her own. Two nurses pulled aside the chained curtain to reveal her hospital room. Their lips waved in silence.

BLOODY MARYANN
EMMA MACLEOD

I glance down at my bloodied hands and it's not Brittany Richardson, head cheerleader and the most popular girl in school that stares back at me, not blinking and not breathing, that makes me realize what I've done. Instead, it's the almost silent and slow drip of the blood exiting her head now that shoots me right back into my body. I drop the state championship trophy with a dull thud at my feet. I back up so the growing pool of blood doesn't touch my pristine white cheer sneakers.

I feel nothing inside, no guilt, no pain, as I pick up my crimson bow from the ground and adjust it back into my hair. I walk to the locker room mirror with no urgency or worry and I wash my hands of Brittany Richardson's blood, surveying my makeup as I do so. My hand twitches a few times as I readjust my high ponytail.

Bitch who are you calling bitch, Brittany Richardson?

I clean up my lipstick.

I'm done with these petty games.

I make sure to rub the blood fingerprints off my bow with my thumb till it disappears into the fabric.

I'll show you.

I slam my clean hands down on the counter and take a deep breath.

Well, that was quite the adrenaline rush.

I am now as perfect as my white cheer sneakers and I walk out of the locker room like every other cheerleader here and back to the gymnasium to continue to cheer for the Everglade Highschool basketball game. We were awarded a 5-minute bathroom break thanks to our hard work on the sidelines of this game.

I seem to have used my time wisely.

I saunter over to the group of cheerleaders at the front row of the bleachers and like clockwork Margo Smith spins on her heels to scowl at me.

"Where have you been MaryAnn? That was six minutes not five." She snaps.

Usually, at this moment, I would be tense and apologetic, but I am nothing but calm with Margo Smith, the little minion of Brittany Richardson.

At least, she was.

"MaryAnn are you even listening to me?" Margo Smith half shrieks. "I want an explanation for why you took so fucking long."

"Margo, it's sixty extra seconds. Don't get your pom poms in a twist,"

Margo Smith's mouth opens and closes, she's barely even heard me say a word other than apologizing when I do something like breathing. A small smile spreads onto my face watching one of the girls who terrorized me now speechless. I wipe the smile off my face before more people see it.

"Now shouldn't we be doing our job?" I ask.

"We um, we can't," Margo Smith stutters. "Brittany isn't back yet."

And she will never be back.

"She's probably talking to some boy," I huff. "You're second in command, aren't you?"

"Well, uh, yes I am."

I take a step forward to her not close enough to be in her face but enough for her to know I mean business.

"I suggest you take control before I do," I whisper. Standing there face to face with Margo Smith, something begins my heart racing, I'm not sure what it is. But the only thing going through my head is how easy it would be to slip my hands on her neck and hold her till she too stopped breathing. But maybe that's a plan for another time.

Right now the most important thing I have to do is cheer and maybe if I cheer loud enough, I'll catch the attention of Bryce Archer, the point guard on the basketball team, super-hot and super popular. There was a rumor floating around for a while that Bryce Archer and Brittany Richardson had a thing but that couldn't possibly be true. I'm watching him dribble up the court right now, so smart, so precise. No guy like him would go out with a she-devil like her. Besides, real or rumor, I think that was squashed today.

I'm so focused on Bryce Archer making a three-pointer and making sure I am the loudest and prettiest voice he hears that I don't see Margo Smith slip out of the gym, but I do when she comes running back in, screaming, tears on her cheeks, high bleach blonde ponytail no longer perfect, bow nearly falling out of her hair, and blood on her white cheer sneakers.

I half skip down the hallway to cheer practice. Since the basketball game last week, it seems like I am the only neon pink crayon in this otherwise white crayon box. The cops have been working hard on their investigation of Brittany Richardson, it seems to have everyone on edge.

Well…almost everyone.

So, I have taken it upon myself to try and calm down the cheer squad before our practice with some yummy almond flour chocolate chip cookies I made myself. By the time I get into the gym, a few minutes late, the mats are already rolled out and all the girls are sitting in a circle tying their not so white cheer sneakers. Margo Smith's pair still has a faint shadow of blood on them. She looks up at me as soon as she finishes tying her sneakers and pushes herself off the ground.

"MaryAnn, are you ever going to even try to make it on time?" She says each word stern, sharper than the next. "Cause I am honestly sick of the late bullshit."

That's when my hands begin to shake, a numbness spreading across my body as I form a tight smile.

"I had a free period so I went home and baked cookies for everyone, I was a little late because of that. I thought everyone could use a little pick me up." I say cheerfully, not letting Margo Smith get to me.

She won't be getting to me anymore.

I pop off the Tupperware lid and push it towards her.

"I know you need the most pick me up out of us all. Please pick the first one." Her eyes grow a little wider, Margo Smith cannot resist a good cookie, her midsection gives that away with her small tummy sticking out from her high waisted lulu lemons. Her greedy fingers grab two cookies and she has them both almost completely eaten by the time I give a cookie to another girl. Once everyone has received a cookie, Margo Smith claps her hands to signal the start of practice.

And to signal her last practice.

Although Margo Smith is not the lightest of our girls, she has always been hell-bent on being a flyer and now that Brittany Richardson is out of the way, she is now top of the pyramid. The place I should be and I have always been alternate for. Instead, here I am in my same stupid spot trying to balance on one foot and prepare myself to catch Margo Smith's chubby ass.

I could just "miss" the catch.

Sadly, instinct takes over as she gets thrown in the air and I catch her flawlessly like I always did with Brittany Richardson. But Margo Smith's balance began to waver. She starts to cough, gross thick coughs. And then a geyser erupts from her mouth and everyone at once drops her and runs. I hit the ground on my ass just like Margo Smith does as she continues to vomit and wheeze. Her eyes are glossy and eyelids droopy.

A few girls rush to Margo Smith's side to try and help any way they can, our coach on the phone with 911. It's no use when Margo's wheezing stops altogether and she falls face down in her own vomit. I leave the mat to keep my cheer sneakers clean.

"She stopped breathing!" Kelly Ortiz yells to our coach.

"Everyone leave the gym now!" Our coach yells and we all obey, I slip my Tupperware of the last of my almond flour chocolate chip cookies and walk past my coach still on the phone.

"She only has two allergies that I know, and she would never consume. Tomatoes and what was the last one." My coach says desperately trying to think.

"Almonds," I add.

"Right thank you MaryAnn." She gives me an attempt at a smile. "And Almonds"

Checkmate. Margo Smith. Check fucking mate.

PUNISHMENT
MAX CARREY

Beck

"*This* is what you were planning?" I ask Jacob, crossing my arms, and feeling tension pinch my brows together. "To break into school?"

"Hey, hey, hey!" a voice shouts. I turn and see Jeremy, with the ever tagalong Dan, walking up across the darkened parking lot. Occasionally to be illuminated by pockets of light from the towering lamps overhead.

Seeing them boils me up, so I put my back to Jacob. "*They're* here too."

"Hey, don't be mad at me okay?" he begs, ambling around and squatting down to put his pleading face in my vision. I set mine even more firmly, which causes him to huff a little murky cloud of air into the chilly night. "Don't be like *this*..."

"Like what?" I snap.

"Like a bummer," Jeremy laughs, Dan sniggering, as they

reach us. Staring with their usual smug faces, makes me want to punch them. My fingers burn, and I curl them into a fist, but my reaction only seems to intensify their amusement.

"Come on baby," Jacob begins cooingly as he attempts to grab hold of my hands, but I yank them away. His lip curls: "God, the boys are right."

"Why? Because *I* don't want to break the rules... the law? What are you planning on doing in there anyway?"

"Mr. Brook's got that big test coming up," Jeremy remarks casually.

"You want to *cheat*?"

"God Beck don't be so sour... Come on, let's go," Jacob orders, walking away toward the front gate with Jeremy and Dan in tow.

My nerves explode. "You can't just leave me out here!"

"Then *come on*." He throws a smug look my way and regret courses through me. *This* is what I get for liking the bad boys. God I'm just like my mother.

"Jacob, I want to go home."

He raises his hand high in the air and presses a button on his fob. His truck lights flood around my black silhouette on the pavement, and then in a flash it's gone. I know he's locked the truck. *Damn!*

My heart begins to pound madly, but my bottom lip trembles as I suddenly feel so vulnerable to all the things that could be lurking in the night. I *need* to get home. I reach a hand into my back pocket, and find no weight there. "You're a bastard! My phone was in there."

Jeremy and Dan have already hurdled themselves over the gate with satisfied looks on their disgusting faces, and my stupid boyfriend hops up, weaving his fingers through the links in the gate to follow. But he pauses to shout back to me: "Then come on inside and use one of the phones in here to call the police on us," and then climbs over.

"Ahhh!" I half scream half growl, as I stomp over to them. "Once this night is over Jacob you and me, we're through."

Jacob throws me a confident smirk that I used to mistake as a handsome passion for me, but now I see it's just for himself. "Who knows, perhaps you'll learn to live a little and then *thank* me for it later."

I spit at him through the chain links, but Jacob just wipes a hand over his face with a laugh.

"Spicy," Jeremy remarks haughtily.

I narrow my eyes into daggers and direct them his way, but it doesn't keep his cocky face from shining with superiority. I should have known better. Never judge them by how they are with only you, judge them by how they are around their friends...grandma used to say. She was smart, I think as I begin to climb the gate, unlike stupid me.

I make my way over, luckily landing light on my feet, instead of face planting on the cement. The entrance is empty, but lit for "security" purposes, all the good that seems to do. Shadows dance along the hallways, cascading across the façade of classrooms, and echoing along the corridors. My spine tingles and I shiver, but rub my arms as if I'm cold so as to not let the boys see my fright.

"Let me borrow your cell," I say.

"No," Jacob replies tersely.

"Don't even think it," Jeremy teases me, and Dan is nodding his head back and forth no.

"I swear to God I'm going to-"

"What? What're you going to do about it?" Jacob says as he lets anger ripple through his face. "Three against one, you're not getting our phones. You're going to have *find* one in there." He points toward the school.

My feet want me to climb back over the gate, but I can't leave. Home is too far away, and it's several lonely blocks to the convenience store, which doesn't seem safe this late at night. Neither does going up to a stranger's house and knocking on their door, hoping they aren't some creep. As much I hate *them*, I'm safest with them.

Holding my head high, as if the murky mouth of the school doesn't run icy fire through my veins, I say: "Fine let's get this over with."

Dan

I feel bad because Beck seems more than uncomfortable, she looks furious... I don't blame her, but I can't *do* anything. I finally got in the popular circle. I can't piss Jeremy and Jacob off. Next thing I know I'd be shoved into lockers or have my head forced down into the toilet. No, she's just going to have to suck it up.

"How are we getting in?" she asks.

Jacob pulls out a slender silver tool with a shit eating grin on his face. "With this."

"You've got a lock pick?"

"I-"he begins but Jeremy cuts him off.

"I don't think we'll be needing that."

We all rush over to the door and see that its handle is lopsided and hanging loosely.

"Alright," Jacob high five's Jeremy, putting away the lock pick.

"Guys, I don't think this is a good idea... what if someone's here," Beck whines.

"Would you stop being such a scaredy cat? It's probably been like this forever, everyone's too lazy here to give a shit," Jacob snaps, then splays a crooked grin on his face. "My lady, your phone awaits."

She growls and storms past, with us following behind. Our footsteps echo against the linoleum and my eyesight is fuzzy against the shadowy blobs that line the walls. I swear I can see them move, but I rub my eyes and continue on, ignoring their vibrations.

"It's down here!" Jeremy shouts, and we all go running to Mr. Brooke's classroom.

When we burst in the light from the window illuminates the chalk board, yesterday's equation is still written on it. The room is murky, and the empty seats look foreboding, as if bodies still sit there, but I just can't see them. A gnawing ache gnashes at my stomach.

Beck rushes forward to the phone on the desk as Jacob starts looking for the test, digging through drawers. But she's gone deathly pale in the moonlight, "Guys, the phone's dead. I'm not getting a dial tone."

"Bingo!" Jacob shouts, his teeth glinting in the blackness. He pulls out a bunch of papers shuffling through it. "This is it."

Jeremy is pacing around the room, concocting something, I can tell by the scrunch of his face. "You know, why not take advantage of the situation? Let's get the chem test too while we're at it!"

A smirk draws Jacob's grin wider. "Brilliant."

Beck's eyes flare. "Did you not hear me? The phone is dead!"

"Okay, okay," he exhales roughly, rolling his eyes. "Why don't you go with them, and look for another phone?"

She snarls and her expression twists up sourly at our mention.

"Or why don't you just wait it out, huh? We'll be outta here in no time."

"Or you could give me your cell or your keys-" she mumbles.

Jacob straightens his back, looming over her, pointing a harsh index finger at her. "Why've you got to ruin everything? Just shut up. Shut up! Shut up! Let *us* do what we came here to do?"

Her mouth is agape, before she pinches her lips together into a firm line. Beck goes over to a seat and plops herself down in it, staring at the desk, mumbling under her breath further: "what *you* came here to do."

Jeremy smirks at Beck, "If the show is done now," turning to Jacob, "we'll go to the labs."

Jacob greedily looks over the answer sheet. His smile turns devilish, unnaturally wide, into Cheshire cat territory.

I follow Jeremy quietly, dutifully as always. Listening to him drone on about Beck, but hearing none of it, for the darkness is creeping, enveloping us...I swear it is. It's lashing out at our heels, and licking with barbed tongues. I've never liked the dark, but something about *this* dark sets my soul to terror. I can feel myself soaking through my shirt with sweat, my breaths are shallow, and everything around me pulsates, as I refuse to blink, trying to catch the *something* traveling in it. God, I don't even *need* to be here. My grades are good, though I wouldn't let anyone know, because cool people don't try too hard. Though I think I try harder now than I ever have.

"Here we are," Jeremy presents in a TV host sort of voice as we reach the labs.

I go to laugh to appease him, but I can feel hot breath brush against the nape of my neck. I whip around, squeaking my shoes, trembling inside them.

"What?" Jeremy asks frustrated.

The pits of darkness swell up and down the hall. Anxiety sparks to fire inside me, acid churning its way up into my mouth. "There's *someone* here..." I whisper.

"Geez man, you-"

But he's cut short. A grating noise pulls its way from the end of the hall toward us, approaching slowly. Dread grasps hold over me and I feel frozen. The grating is slicing, chunky, like something sharp is dragging along the wall, heavily.

"What the f-"

The darkness bulges around a blackened form. A shoulder peaks out from obscurity, highlighted by the trickle of light. *Someone's* there!

"Hello?!" Jeremy calls out, and I can hear his voice brake a little.

The grating stops, the figure immobile. *He* lulls his head to the side, unveiling it to the light. Buzzed cut hair, rough reddened skin where shadows etch it severely. One manic eye is open wide, exposing all the glistening wetness of white, around a skinny slit of black pupil. A chill shakes me. My eyes waver as the man lulls back into the darkness.

"Oh my god," Jeremy says with a hallowed out voice. "It's-"

Suddenly the shadows swell, engorged, and the grating picks up pace, footsteps running, slamming against the floor, echoing in my ears.

"Run!" Jeremy shouts, and I can hear his footsteps retreating.

My body goes to move, but I wrench in place. Not able to move my feet, my knees go weak, and I feel myself shrinking to the floor. The sounds grow larger, enveloping me.

"Come on man!" Jeremy calls.

But I'm shivering, freezing, with white static fuzzing over my brain. The noise is almost painful, ringing with fury. Approaching, expanding into a symphony of crunching, pulverizing plaster. Then suddenly the noise ends, cut short.

"Dan," Jeremy's voice slithers to me.

No, no... the shadows seem slimmer, not as bloated, as if it'd been a snake that had swallowed an entire body and finally digested it. But my fragmented mind is still blistering with each sudden noise, movement... hot breath wisps across my bare wrists. *He's still here!*

The soles of my feet begin to melt, trying to allow me to

run, but a cackle with a broken edge to it punctures the air. A pungent smell of urine overtakes me. A wet heat travels down my leg.

A figure leaps out from the darkness, a twisted hand held high above his head. The skin from his fingers flayed all the way back to his palm. The tendons are torn to shreds, muscle and sinew falling off in bits. The bone and joints of his fingers are filed down, sharpened to deadly points, stiff and resolute. I feel my knees give out, a light fainting overtakes the thudding erratic beating of my heart, and I melt to the floor.

He looks down at me with a glossy wet smile, with inky black spaces where there should be teeth. He strikes forward. The razor sharp points of his fingers melt my skin like butter as he carves through my shoulder blade. Pain searing through me, the air stinging my raw flesh, my throat heaves with a scream but I can't even hear it.

Jeremy

His blood sprays out, flinging through the air, as McGregor's claw slashes across his chest. Blood dots and splatters the linoleum that burst red in the light. Dan collapses to the ground, squirming. Five jagged gashes cut deeply in his flesh. His shrieks issue forth, pinging off my eardrums hauntingly.

"Get up!" I shout, tears welling my eyes. My blood pools at my fingertips and toes, the sound of it rushing in my ears.

McGregor draws back his crimson stained hand. My stomach lurches. Dan twists and pulls himself toward me by his forearms. His face is unrecognizable, so warped in fear.

"Help me!" he screams.

"Ingrates!" McGregor's voice reverberates inside the agonizing wails. "You're an infection, diseasing this school, contaminating the brightest of minds."

McGregor sends a kick into his side. And he flips over,

breathless, splayed out. I wince against his tearful sobs, sucking in the thick sickly sweet air. McGregor lifts his knee up to his chest and brings his foot down on Dan's ribcage. Loud cracking and pops pair with blood spurting out through gritted teeth, like a tormented fountain. Then he's wheezing, jerking, against the pulverizing movements, as McGregor grinds down on his heel. Dan's body twitches unnaturally.

My eyes fog over and streams run down my face, my veins bubble with throbbing adrenaline. I turn and run, leaving them behind.

McGregor's voice travels with me up the hall, "Time for your punishment!"

My feet carry me, raggedly back the way I'd come, and I almost collide into Jacob and Beck.

"What the hell was that?" he asks. "What's going on?"

"Dan's dead!"

Jacob sputters out in a laugh. Anger courses through me, igniting a fire in my belly. I grasp him by his shirt and body slam him up against the wall. His face begins to screw up, but my words unhinge it.

"He's *dead*! It's McGregor!"

Confusion washes over him, but I can also see an icy fear and he tenses. "Principal McGregor?"

"Yeah man, we gotta get out of here," I peel myself off him, but as I go to run Jacob grabs a fistful of my jacket and pulls me back, so that I swing around and he slams me into the wall. "Let me go!" I yell, trying to flail out of his hold, but he sends his forearm across my chest, digging an elbow into my shoulder and forcing the other down with his meaty hand. I cry, "We're all going to die."

"You high? McGregor's locked up in a mental institution."

"No, he must have escaped; you've got to believe me."

"The broken lock, the dead phone," Beck mumbles. Her eyes are huge watery discs in the muddy light. She's holding herself. I've hated her since day one, a tight wound up bitch, but now things seem a whole hell of a lot different. I feel sorry for her, sorry how I've been to her. She spasms, "Who *is* he?"

"Our killer if we don't get out of here," I grunt as I throw up a knee and send it between Jacob's legs, he releases me and curls to the floor. I grab Beck's hand. "He's coming after us-"

"No," I'm cut off by a deep burly voice, *"he's already here."*

Stabbing pain lurches through me. I jolt forward, but am kept in place, spasming. Beck gasps. Jacob is scuttling away. My nerves ripple in waves, my veins running cold. I look down and see five glistening red tips protruding from my gut. Blood drenches my shirt, pooling down to the floor. McGregor's breath steamy on the back of my ear.

"Time for *your* punishment!"

"No!" Beck screams, trying to pull me away with her, yanking at my arm, but I let her go and the force of it sends her hurling back.

"Run, get out of he-" I stop, my voice transforming into cries as McGregor rips his hand downward, slicing into my stomach. I feel of burning liquid, spilling out, as my body convulses. My limbs go limp, my mind cloudy... my vision cutting to black.

Jacob

Jeremy's stomach is torn to shreds, his innards slopping out. Purple tinted intestine tumbles onto the linoleum, as his eyes flicker behind closed lids, then shutter to a stop. His empty husk is tossed aside. Blood oozes out, and his stomach bile tries to seep into it, but the green sits on top like rancid olive oil.

Next thing I know Beck is pulling on me. "Jacob!"

McGregor steps over Jeremy's body, cocking his head to the side, he cracks his neck. His wide but beady eyes are burrowing into my skull. The blood vessels against his pale iris branch out like a twisted tree. My prickly nerves sting me.

I tuck my feet in and scramble up. Beck drags me into the classroom next to us by my wrist, and I can feel my joint buckle against her pull.

McGregor charges, stomping toward us.

Beck lets out a battle cry and slams the door, locking it. But suddenly the knob flicks about madly. I start with each clatter of the metal. She pushes me to the side and I fall limply over, my eyes transfixed on the door. I feel her hand in my pocket. My heartbeat is ringing in my ears. Tears cascade down my face to drip off my chin. I'm quivering with fear, dread filling me up with a glacial weight.

Suddenly it stops. The door is no longer shimmying against the frame. The metal is silent and still.

"We need help!" she whispers urgently. I whip my head around to see she's on my cellphone, but my eyes nervously flick back to the door. "There's someone trying to kill us. We're in Sandston High.... Hello? *Hello?* Shit."

I sit up, twitching. "But you-you got through. They're coming...they're going to come and save us."

"It's not like in the movies Jacob," her mouth drags down into a frown, her brow pinching together, her hands trembling and she drops my phone making me jump. "It could take five, ten minutes, or more."

"No, no no no no no..." I cry, backing up into the wall, pushing until I'm flush with it. I bury my face in my hands. Collecting my tears inside my palms and as I heave I can taste the salt. I must have bit myself because I can also taste iron, and it runs slickly down my throat.

"Jacob, Jacob..." trying to get my attention, "*who* is that out there?"

"He-he..." I begin but break down into heavier sobs.

"I need to know who we're up against Jacob... He killed Jeremy..." her voice hitches, "Dan."

I tear my face from my hands. I can feel a heat rise in my cheeks, as I stutter: "H-he-he was the principal before you showed up. He jammed a pencil into a kid's eyeball, all the way up into his brain."

"Oh my god," she sputters with a ragged breath. "Why?"

"*I* don't know! The twisted fucker enjoyed it, obviously."

She nods her head, her glittering eyes shifting to far away into the depths of the gloomy room, thinking. "We need to figure out what to do."

"No, no no... We're staying here. We'll be safe... he can't get in-"

Just then a metallic scraping comes from outside. The wiggling, jangling, grows ever fervent. I look to Beck, barely able to make out her silhouette amidst the smoky blackness. She looks spurred into action while my muscles feel sore and heavy.

"He's trying to get in....he's picking the lock...the lock!" She slides over on her knees, jamming her hand in my pocket again, pulling out the slim silver tool. Grabbing a fist full of my collar she yanks me. "We need to get behind the door."

I sluggishly crawl after her, positioning myself beside her. The grating is prickling my skin, goose bumps rising to chilly bumps. The sound is deafening, it's unnatural...it's bone against metal. I can picture him jimmying the lock with a filed finger.

"When he opens the door-"

I seep to the floor crying.

"*When* he does, I'm going to stab him in the foot, then we're going to run past him okay?"

I shake my head.

"We don't have a choice Jacob."

Beck brings up her hand, knuckles tightly wrapped

around the pick. Her whole body is tensed, on the edge, while I'm melting into the chilly embrace of the shadows, sinking further in the linoleum.

CLICK

A brittle snap, then a metallic pull. All is deathly quiet as the knob begins to turn. Then the door pushes open with a suctioned pop. McGregor wraps his spikey hand around the corner of the door, his index finger's tip has splintered off, left in jagged shards. The acid in my stomach boils, popping nervous bubbles. His bare foot steps into sight. Beck brings down her arm, the pick puncturing the vulnerable flesh, sinking down with a *chink* to the floor. A blood curdling yell, as scarlet bursts from the wound.

Just as he topples forward Beck yells: "Now!"

She yanks the door fully open and lurches to run, but McGregor's cold eyes latch onto me, causing my feet to burn spurring me to flight. I shove Beck out of the way and run ahead of her. My clumsy stomps echo throughout the hall. My lungs are afire, I can barely catch breath. I'm almost at the door that leads to freedom, when I glance back. Beck's stumbling out of the classroom, heading off in the opposite direction. McGregor's up, practically toppling forward, leaning against the door frame. Beck is so close to him, an easy target. But I don't care, it's every man for himself.

My hand wraps around the loose knob, and I can taste the victory on my tongue. Yet as I wriggle it refuses to budge. I start slamming my weight against it, and can see it squirm against the frame. Yet it won't dislodge. *He's* barred the exits. I hear a scrapping noise approach. When I flick my eyes behind McGregor fills my vision. The shadows lick across his body, dancing across his rough edges. His eyelids are drawn back into deeply set sockets, and weathered smoking lines trace his smiling lips. He crookedly walks to me, limping with his damaged foot. Red prints trailing him. Relentless.

"Why *me*?" I shout. Tears fog over his visage. I can feel myself begin to shrink. "She was right there! You can still catch her..." I whine. "Just p-p-please...leave *me* alone."

A haughty laugh bounces off the slick floors and cool walls. Ringing through my head as it develops into a throaty snarl. "Why, you're the worst of them all, *aren't* you?"

McGregor spews hot breath in my face. A rancid sticky sweet odor invades my senses. He raises his shattered finger, pieces of fractured bone. He draws it forward but I swipe at the air droopily, drained of energy. McGregor toys with me, letting me swat him away, chuckling darkly. I dissolve further into myself and he takes the opportunity to strike out. The splintered bone ruptures my fragile skin. Blood trickles down my throat.

"Scream for me," he growls. Suddenly he saws the splinters through my windpipe. I burble screams that drown in blood. My body retching. Sprays of crimson drench McGregor's gaunt face. My eyes flicker back into my skull. Seizing up, twitching in agony. He reaches in, his hand burrowing into my neck. Plucking something that doesn't want to give, until he slices it to shreds. I wilt into him, fading to black.

Beck

Sliding frantically across the floor I hurdle myself toward the teacher's chair. Pulling it by an armrest around the desk, I hear Jacob's muffled screams and it pitches my heart into my throat. I start, letting go of the chair and it rolls until thudding against the wall. I feel frozen to the spot, my feet becoming encased in ice, "Snap yourself out of it," I say. Nodding wildly. I swallow my heart back into place and force my feet to move.

Grasping hold of the chair I take to the window at a run, chucking it at the last second. It crashes through, clattering glass, a huge gaping hole in its wake. A cold burst of air hits me, and it tastes fresh, unlike the thick murky haze of the school. I lunge at it, at the broken pieces of glass still lodged in the frame. Jumping half my body through, my skin and clothes catch on the jagged sharp edges, tearing into me. I grit my teeth and continue to push through, ignoring the cutting heat. My foot hits cement... then a searing pain overtakes my arm, like several large needles have all sunk into me. I look behind and see McGregor's claw dug into my flesh. I tug against it to tear myself free, but he pulls back slinging me from the window.

I hit the floor head first. My brain rattles around my skull, and white stars spark in my vision. Little shards of glass are embedded into my flesh, some completely lost in it, and a bigger shard is wedged into my thigh. I moan, as I try to scramble up, but instead am kept down by the crushed tendon. Overly tensed, seeping blood, the glass burning into me. My trembling hands go to remove it, but I hesitate, then decide to leave it in. I slap my hand uselessly down to the floor beside me and hit something wet. I see red coat my fingers. There's a long bloody lump lying on the linoleum and when my eyes focus I scream. It's a tongue, with a tattered stump.

"Your friend was saying quite a lot of boorish things," McGregor says casually, slowly stalking toward me. He's framed by the broken window, the moon shining through casts a long menacing shadow. "So I figured he didn't need *that* anymore."

"Why?" I helplessly blurt, unable to move, fearing it would sink the glass in further, cause the bleeding to quicken. "Why do all this? Principals' are supposed to help."

A crooked grin screws up his face. Smirking with indifference at my plight, he walks past me toward the teacher's desk and sits down upon its edge. He slashes through the air, splaying his claw out in front of him. Admiring it, yet frowning at the splintered finger. His voice is low and heady, venom coursing through it. "There was a student who was an imbecile. He got a fellow student, who was bright, to write all his papers for him. Not surprisingly we found out, as no one that *dim* catapults themselves to such a high degree overnight."

He pulls a mechanical pencil sharpener closer towards him and shoves his fractured finger in. The machine shrieks grinding away at bare bone until cutting to a stop. The sound is sickening, making me want to vomit, but I keep focus. I apply as much pressure as I can to wrap my flesh around the glass, keep everything tightly together, still I bleed profusely and it sloshes to the floor. *Any second now, any moment...the cops will come. Keep him talking.* "What happened?"

He arches a patchy eyebrow, narrowing his eyes. Jerking his finger from the sharpener he reveals its crude form. It's shorter but razor-sharp. He blows on it cheekily as if casting off pencil shavings. "That bright boy's future was taken from him. His scholarship ripped away, all because of a *bully*. And he killed himself... it was only *right* that the person responsible was *punished* too."

"The person responsible?" I mutter through shallow breaths. "*You* were the principal, and all that happened right under *your* nose."

"You're right," he replied leaning forward, wincing. Little, drop, drop, drops are decorating underneath from his wounded foot. His claw-like hand tremors from the violence of the sharpener. "That's why I have to punish the bad before they infect the good. Which reminds me...what are *you* doing here so late at night?"

"I didn't want to come, they *made* me."

He clucks his tongue. "Now, now, now...don't be a liar. I already know you're a *cheat*."

"No," I plead exasperated. "I'm telling the truth. You don't want to be *wrong* do you? Let another... innocent bullied kid pay do you?" I say all too sweetly.

"No, I suppose not, but you see..." his grin turns devilish, the corners spreading to his ears, "*he* gave up when the going got rough, *he* wasn't as bright as I thought as he was. You've got to fight for what you want... It's the principal of the thing after all."

His joints seem to coil, and then abruptly spring forward. I send out a kick with my good leg, hitting him squarely in the gut, hurling him back. My left arm is crumpled into my chest, but with my other elbow I begin to pull myself. I army crawl while on my back against the slick floor. It's slow and I screech against the pain. All my muscles tense, wriggling the glass in my thigh. The white stars start to explode in my vision again. McGregor appears like fireworks are bursting all about him as he charges forward. I'm barely able to pull myself through the doorframe. Jacob's dead body greets me back out in the hall. *This is it... I'm going to die.*

McGregor lands on his knees, leaning over me manically. Claw poised in the air, he brings it down... I wrench my wounded arm up to block my face. His fingers sink through again. Raw, throbbing, tender flame ignites me. Trembling I fight to keep my arm up, for the sharp tips of bone have broken through and hover mere inches from my throat. My arm wavers and begins to dip in the air, I rumble up a yell as I snatch my wrist with my opposite hand to keep it up. I brace myself for him to put his full weight onto me, but instead McGregor's smile softens into interest.

"You really *are* a fighter..." he utters slowly.

Sirens sound in the distance. Tires crumble on the pavement outside. Colors flashing through the broken window paint the walls red and blue.

"Ah...the cavalry," he snarls, his face regaining its cruel twist. He pulls back, yanking his claw free. I cry, my arms tumbling to my chest. Yet he raises a closed fist above my head.

"No," I say breathlessly as he sends it forward and smashes it into my face. Blackness...

I jolt up with a start. My heart beating madly against my ribs, my body screaming it's soreness, but there's lights, a clean white room, and beneath me is a mattress, beside me tubes, monitors, a cast on my arm. Flicking blankets back I see my thigh is bandaged. A shrill beeping fills the air. The door flicks open, and I tense, almost expecting to see McGregor but instead there's a short woman wearing scrubs, her voice echoing out to others behind her, "She's awake!"

Suddenly my mother tramples in, her eyes bloodshot and her hands stretch out to me. I wince picturing McGregor's filed down fingers dripping blood. "Oh baby," she murmurs embracing me. "My poor baby, how do you feel?"

I sink into her, wedging my face into the crook of her neck. "*He* killed them," I sob. "He killed them all!"

I wrench myself back and see a woman standing in the corner. She's wearing a plain slate gray suit, and she's studying me with intense scrutiny. Her eyes narrow... and they're McGregor's for a brief flickering moment... then her brows pinch together. "Who?" she whispers but it echo's in my eardrums.

My mom is shuffled off to the side as the nurse flashes a light into my eyes, though my gaze doesn't shift off the woman. The nurse fiddles with the machines. "It looks as if you're doing fine, but I'm going to go get the Doctor, okay?" she says scuttling off.

My mom hugs me again, but I suck in a sharp breath through gritted teeth. She goes ridged and backs away mumbling, "Sorry, sorry..." her eyes are watery, and her face is blotchy red. "Oh baby...what happened?"

"*He's dead! It's McGregor!*" Jeremy's voice remerges in my head. Then his body's impaled, I'm trying to yank him free, but he let's go as McGregor shreds his stomach open. *Jacob...* throat slit, slumped over in the hall against the door. Tongue removed.... I remember the feel all too well and it sends a shiver down my spine. It's spongy texture, slick with blood.

The flashes of memory cease for a moment, and I lift my head to gaze at the woman in the corner. A shinny badge is clipped onto her belt. I inhale and hold it, trying to steady myself. "It was McGregor," I say on exhale. "The old principal."

Her eyes go wide, the whites of them unnervingly stark. "We were not able to apprehend any suspects at the scene."

"*He* got away?" I cry, a shiver courses through me, and I can feel delicate points tip toe up my neck, imagining McGregor's pale bony fingers. "*They...*" I choke, "said he must have escaped from-"

"Saint Peregrine's," the woman finishes absolutely, her face setting firmly. She nods in thought. "A fire broke out at the institution this morning. It's believed that he died along with several others."

My mother digs her nails into my wrists, her mouth hanging open, and my tremble seems to have infected her. She shakes terribly, yet is ridged, looking as if she might snap herself in half.

"You *have* to believe me," I sputter desperately to them both. "He's out there..." A chill overtakes me. The grating of his finger in the pencil sharpener blasts in my ears to haunt me. "...and he's looking to exact punishment."

ASHES, ASHES
MICAELA MICHALK

In the distance, a coyote was howling. Callie used to relish these summer nights and the music the evenings brought. Something tonight was missing to the usual symphony, though. The locust joined the chorus in the trees and a cool gentle breeze made the windchimes on the porch ding in rhythm, but the clouds darkened the sky, obfuscating the stars. It was a new moon. Callie shivered. She wasn't sure if it was the darkness that seemed to swallow her that made her feel empty. It probably had to do more with the fact of what she'd done earlier that day, but the sky and the darkness... that was easier to focus on.

She wasn't sure how long she stood there in her front yard, staring up at the abyss. The streetlights were broken, some still flickering on and off. In between their blinks, Callie wondered if the darkness could envelop the whole world. It was this thought that got her walking. As a preteen, she found the nights exciting, running from bonfire to bonfire.

The flames would flare towards the sky, as if to become stars themselves. Her friends sang country songs around the circle. Despite the fact they lived more towards the north, they seemed to always pretend they were cowboys. Now, walked the black paved roads, skipping over the potholes where the ground sank. There were no friends. No fire.

Callie's hand shook, despite the breeze having settled. Another coyote joined the howling; they sounded closer. Callie clutched her stomach, fighting the urge to throw up. She never wanted to be near fire again. Not after what happened earlier, what she did. It was an accident; she swore to herself. They would never believe her, though. "It was an accident," she said aloud to herself, to the empty world where only the creatures could hear. It scared her to think she might be lying. The thought left her mind as quickly as it entered. She couldn't confront that.

Callie continued to walk, not sure where her legs were carrying her. All the houses she passed were dark without so much as a candle in the window. Vaguely, she wondered what time it was. She must have been lost in this darkness for hours. Or, it could have only been minutes. Still, she walked. The only things that followed her were the sounds of the animals: an owl hooting and a branch creaking to the tune of a forgotten lullaby.

She was desperate not to blink. Even when the breeze started up again and stung her eyes, Callie resolved to keep them open. She wasn't afraid of the shadows around her, nor the wild animals that lurked just beyond the town's limits. She did wonder if they encroached upon human territory at night when they were sleeping. But her worst fear was not the confrontation of a coyote. It was what she saw when her eyes were closed. Yet, her resolution to always keep them open only lasted a few minutes. When they watered against the chilly air and an eyelash found its way through her lid, she succumbed, squinting in pain. As her eyes squeezed shut, the images she failed to dissuade came at her like bullets, hammering into her vision one after one.

The sun hitting the cornfield behind the bar in a way that made the stalks gleam ripe. The abandoned cabin the town council still hadn't taken down and the adults warned to stay away from because of the asbestos. Callie knew they were lying to keep the teens out of trouble. The cabin was built with old dogwood logs. The teenagers used the place to smoke marijuana after school, and the walls indeed were crumbling with mold. In the summer, it became Callie and her friend's meeting place, ever since they were twelve. They would share secrets, drink beer, and hook up with boys their parents would never approve of. Callie kept her eyes shut longer than necessary; she felt as if she were transported to the cabin. Like she could smell cedar and pine and a hint of corn. Her back ached where she scratched it earlier, having crawled through the open spot in the boarded windows. In the shadows of the cabin room, her friend, Esther, had been waiting. When her half-shadowed face appeared in Callie's vision, Callie forced her eyes open.

It was an accident, Esther. Callie thought it like a prayer, as if her thoughts could carry up to heaven and the angels would believe her. She dug her nails into her palms, pinching the skin that held her sins so deeply within. A mosquito landed on her arm, but she didn't brush it away, even as his mouth sucked her dry. Her legs ached against the exertion as she kept walking, away from the neighborhoods. Callie suddenly knew where she was taking herself. Towards the cornfields. She couldn't bring herself to turn back, though.

There was one more house before the cabin, set apart from the neighborhoods because it was bigger. Not quite a mansion but not a simple house either. No one really knew who lived there. A wealthy town recluse. The Boo Radley of the North, some used to say. There was one light on in the attic window and as Callie passed, it switched off. An owl hooted its goodnight and Callie's stomach sank further.

There should be fireflies out, Callie reflected. They would give her light but then again, she didn't want the implications their thoraxes would bring. She didn't know where they were hibernating this night, but Callie was jealous of their comfort. For they were together, wherever they were. Callie hunched her shoulders as the wind picked up faster. It may have been summer, but the night seemed very cold.

When Callie crawled in the cabin earlier, she wasn't expecting Esther's fury. The way Esther pouted her lips and her curly hair bounced aggressively on her shoulders. She had her arms crossed over her heavyset chest, holding an unlit cigarette in one hand. Dutifully, Callie had handed her the lighter she always carried in her pocket. Despite accepting the offering and putting the end of her cig aflame, Esther had scowled at Callie the whole time.

After taking a drag of smoke, she looked at her friend with disdain. "I know what you did." Her words were venom, each syllable punctuated with hate.

"It wasn't me," Callie had said, lighting her own cigarette. Smoke had calmed her then. It reminded her of barbecues and childhood. "It was my dad."

"Your dad got my dad fired, but we know you're the thief." Callie wasn't expecting Esther to blow a face full of smoke into her face. She had coughed, gripping the burning end of her cigarette. She felt ash on her skin.

Between coughs, Callie tried to vomit the words out. "I...didn't...steal...anything." She knew Esther wasn't angry because her dad got caught embezzling money from the business. She was angry because she hooked up with the same guy earlier that month. Esther never said they were exclusive, and best friends were supposed to share.

Esther wrinkled her nose. "Where did you get the lighter then?" She asked, handing it back.

Callie took it in her hands but didn't respond. She fixed her eyes on it and the gold plus sign logo against the smooth black background. She did steal the lighter two years back from the big Boo Radley house. She had snuck in on a dare and snatched it as proof. It was her first but not her last swipe.

Esther stuck her nose up at Callie's silence. "You rob everything. Lighters, boys, money. You robbed my family of its future. I should never have been friends with a maniac like you. I should have believed everyone who said not to trust the daughter of a murderer."

When Esther said those words, Callie's blood had boiled. She felt as if she had sent the cigarette right to her bloodstream. "My mother's death was an accident, *you* know that."

Callie's mom fell from the top window of their house seven years ago. If she landed normally, the paramedics said she would have been mostly fine, besides a few broken bones. But she had the misfortune to land on their spiked fence. Callie was just a little girl, playing in the yard then. She heard her mom scream and saw the way the spikes went through her ribcage. She never saw someone bleed from the mouth before nor had she seen someone's arms flail so wildly. Her mom tried to tell her something as she died but her voice was hoarse and every time, she opened it was only blood, not words, that poured out. There was a flock of crows on the roof. Her father cried.

There was an investigation, but it was ruled as an accident. Callie's mom was not pushed. Still, that didn't stop the townspeople from talking. "A psychopath for a Dad, a sociopath for a kid," they said. But it wasn't true. In their small town, they were isolated. Esther had been the only one to stay by Callie's side.

When Esther stared at Callie in the dark cabin, angry brown eyes aglow by the end of her cigarette, she sneered for the first time at her. "Your father is crazy. And so are you."

Callie's fists were tight, and she didn't realize she had been walking with her eyes closed. She unclenched her teeth and tried to control her breathing. It felt like she wasn't getting enough air, like her body was slowly inflating with carbon dioxide until she would explode. Shuddering, she opened her eyes, but she already knew where she was.

The cabin that once stood by the cornfield was now reduced to rubble. Only a few of the supporting beams were left standing and though it was hard to tell in the dark, Callie knew that they, too, were charred. Beneath the pile of ashes and wood, Callie wondered if the bones were still there. She had fled before the fire department came so she did not know if they searched for bodies inside or not. Bile rose up her throat, the acid burning her esophagus as it climbed. It was worse to be forgotten.

Ahead, something seemed to swish in the corn. Callie froze. She did not know if someone other than a scarecrow lived in the fields, but she could not let them see her guilt. A minute passed of silence and Callie relaxed, only slightly. She shook her head to herself. She shouldn't have guilt.

"It was an accident." She repeated to the rubble and the bones beneath. To herself. Yet she fell to her knees in the scorched grass.

When the cabin was still standing, only hours earlier, Esther had called Callie crazy. Her dad a murderer. Callie's hand was shaking with rage as she went to light another cigarette and she was fighting the urge to punch Esther in the face. To break her pretty nose and watch it bleed.

She moved her hand too fast when she was lighting her smoke. *That's* what happened. The lighter flew from her hand towards Esther, onto her precious curls.

"It was an accident," Callie sobbed into the grass, the rubble, and the cornfield. The darkness swallowed her words as if to deny Callie any absolution. It seemed to know the joy Callie got at seeing Esther's hair aflame and hearing the scream curdle the atmosphere. It seemed to know that Callie did nothing to help but stood there, watching as the fire touched Esther's skin, the flesh oozing slowly off her bones.

Callie cried into the land as the darkness called out to her. It wanted her to face one simple truth, perhaps the scariest truth of all.

It was no accident.

DON'T RUN
SYLVIA SON

Stephen lay in bed staring at the ceiling.

Five hours ago he had hit a man with his car.

He kept telling himself it wasn't his fault, that it was an accident.

He had always drove on that intersection with no problem. How was he was supposed to see that guy jaywalk in the middle of the night dashed across the street?

He could still remember the *thunk* noise the jaywalker made when they hit the side of the car and smashed onto the windshield.

He had sat there stunned behind the wheel for minutes staring at the face of the man he had hit unable to think or react.

It was only when he saw the area on the window where the jaywalker's mouth was fogging up that Stephen had realized—the man was still alive.

Stephen pulled the car into reverse and shifted into drive. He thought it would shake the body off. It didn't. Somehow the body remained plastered to the hood of the car and making this horrible gasping and wheezing sounds.

Too much went through his mind. Jail. Death. Just drive drive drive! He didn't know what to do. He kept on driving all the way to his house. He pressed the remote to the garage and slowly drove in and then turned the car off.

The jaywalker still planted on the hood made one last shuddering breath and his body slumped completely still. Stephen counted to 100 before he finally slid out of his seat and maneuvered himself out of the car trying to avoid any part of the dead man's body touching him. He backed out of the garage watching for any second for it to suddenly jump up and lunge at him.

Once he was out of the garage he slowly closed it.

Stephen spent the whole night lying in bed staring at the ceiling. He didn't realize how much time had passed until the clock radio beeped 7:10.

He debated on whether to stay in bed or check the garage.

He decided to check on the body.

He walked down each step with dread, past the kitchen and then to the front door. He didn't bother to put on shoes as he walked out to the garage.

The door was already opened. Did he forget to close it last night? *Oh shit,* he thought. The neighbor would see—

Absolutely nothing.

There should have been a body. And now there was none. Even stranger, the car was completely fine. There were no traces of blood or dents and the windshield was completely fine. Did he dream it all? But he remembered it quite clearly. He remembered the sound of the body hitting the car and that sickening crunch and rack and how the dying man stared at Stephen with such indignation and horror. He couldn't believe he hallucinated the whole thing. He pinched the skin at the back of his hand to remind himself that this was real. He grunted slightly from the pain. It was real.

Good. Grief. You idiot! He said to himself. He smacked himself in the head several times and berated himself for actually complaining. *Do you really want a dead body in your garage? No? Then count this as a small blessing that maybe it was a small animal you had hit.* Just for good measure, he bent down to check under the car. There was nothing there.

"Count yourself lucky," he said out loud. "Maybe it was a dream or a hallucination or it was so late and you were so tired that what you remember was actually a dog or a cat being hit."

Whatever, he was going back to sleep and forget about the last hours.

As he opened the door to go back in he heard a sound coming from the kitchen. It was the heavy *thunk* of his refrigerator door opening then slamming it quite hard.

Terrific. He had avoided a hit-and-run only to end up with a home invasion in his kitchen.

He picked up a hammed in the closet and tiptoed to the room. He raised his hand up and froze.

Sitting in his kitchen table and eating a large bowl of frosted flakes was the man he had hit last night.

And he was a mess. His clothes were ripped in places and covered in blood. His face and neck were covered in bruises, scratches and smears of blood and his nose was smashed in. And there were small pieces of glass were embedded in all around his neck like a collar.

The spoon was still in his mouth when he looked up and saw Stephen standing holding his hammer.

"Oh, good morning," he said. The spoon muffled the words. And once he was aware of that he took it out and repeated himself. "Good morning," he said again.

"I...I thought you were..." The last word was left hanging. He didn't want to say it or else it would make it true.

"Dead?" He lifted up his dirt and blood covered hands. "Yup. You should know. You were there."

Stephen took a step back.

"Hey!" The dead man snapped his fingers several times at him. "Where are you going? Get back here." Then tapped a finger on the table. "Now, sit."

Stephen slowly sat down while the dead man continued to spoon the Frosted Flakes into his mouth with relish. The only sounds in the room were his loud crunching and grunting with pleasure.

He paused for a second. "Oh, this is so good. I'm going to miss this." He kept on spooning every last bit of cereal until there was only the sweetened milk left. And not satisfied, he tilted the bowl up and swallowed down the milk in long and loud gulps.

And once he finished, he exhaled.

"Ah. Now," He belched. "Excuse me. Where were we? Oh, yeah. You had hit me and left me there to die on the hood of you car."

Stephen didn't know what he could say that would make it better.

"I'm sorry?"

The dead man made a small snort of disgust. "Typical," He seemed to be saying this to himself. "They think saying, 'I'm sorry will change things or make it better. But it doesn't." He shook his head. "What are we going to do about it?"

"But..." Stephen said.

"Yes?"

"In my defense," he knew it was a mistake but it was too late to stop. "You shouldn't have jaywalked in the middle of the night."

The dead man didn't speak but stared pure daggers from his eyes.

"Really?"

"Uh...I...Um.." Stephen was sorry. What more did this man want?

"Stop. Talking. I don't want to hear anymore excuses from you." He bent down to reach for something under the table and pulled up a large knife and a hammer and placed them in the middle of the table. "Not. A. Single. Word."

He held the knife in the left hand and the hammer in the right.

"Eh? Eh?" He held the knife up then the hammer in a perverse way of trying to impress Stephen, offering a chance to choose which item to use to kill Stephen with.

Stephen bolted out of the kitchen and the dead man shook his head in disgust.

"Typical," he said. "They always run."

Stephen ran to the garage and tried to open the car door. Shit! He had forgotten his keys! The garage doors slowly lowered, he tried to run before it closed completely but it was too late.

Standing at the side door of the garage was the dead man. He chose to use the hammer and slowly walked towards him.

"You know you're making it hard for me." Stephen doubted the dead man meant he felt emotionally conflicted to kill him, more like how much Stephen was being inconvenient to him. Cornered he grabbed a rake and held it out like a spear.

"Really?" He lifted the hammer.

Stephen screamed and kept on screaming as he rolled off his bed. He only stopped screaming as soon as his face hit the carpeted ground and lay there panting for several minutes.

Once Stephen's breathing finally slowed and evened out, he sat up.

He was in his bedroom.

It was all a dream. A very vivid dream.

He ran downstairs and out the door and pressed the remote.

The garage door took almost forever to lift and once it was finally all the way up Stephen wasn't sure if he wanted it to be real.

Inside, the car was untouched. He felt around the frame and windows to confirm for himself.

After finally exhaling in relief he collapsed next to the car. If he had checked in the side rear view mirror he would have seen the dead man still bloody and bruised walking up behind him lifting the hammer up and bring it down in a slash.

THEY WORE THE SKIN OF THEIR ENEMIES
DONNA J. W. MUNRO

"Lisa, you owe 20,000 words on the Assyrian Conquest article," Daniel growled at her without bothering to face her. She nodded curtly to his back, giving back the rudeness she got. "Hear me? Probably can't through all that blub."

Blub. That's how he'd referred to her weight since she'd started with the company. She, like all the others, tried to keep her head down. Tried to get the work done to collect the check and pay the bills. It was hard to find work as a writer in the first place and this job had been a godsend. If only it weren't for fat-shaming Daniel, the nagging, office asshole.

"Yes, Daniel. I heard." Lisa stretched her fingers against the cramps. She'd typed over 10,000 words toward the goal and had stopped to double check her sources, but Daniel jumped on her the minute she'd paused her typing. He wasn't her boss. It wasn't his job to police her, but he did anyway.

She turned back to the article she was reading, hoping he'd leave her alone.

The details of the Assyrian conquest of Mesopotamia fascinated her. She found the Assyrian conquers liked to wear the people they'd conquered. They'd skin the aristocratic warriors crushed under the spoked wheels of their war chariots. As they passed through the capitol's lapis festooned gates, clattering wheels coated with gore, they let their newly conquered subjects see the sheared away faces dangling as cloaks around their bloodied shoulders. Ghost cloaks made the women weep and the old men collapse against each other's shoulders, a shrugging clutch against the horror.

They only did it with their enemies.

It inspired such fear, Lisa knew, to have your enemies wearing the skins of those you loved.

She settled back in typing on the article, weaving the information artfully.

"Finally," Daniel muttered.

Asshole.

She'd listened to his bullshit for ten months. He'd never been nice to her, picking apart everything she did.

He complained about things her desk.

He bitched about any breaks she took.

He mocked her clothes, her size, even her voice.

The others in the office glanced at her and rolled their eyes, but they never came to her aid.

The Assyrians didn't need to make friends with those they'd conquered. They just needed to keep them in fear. Maybe Daniel was a dick to her because he wanted to keep the others in line. The idea that she was the skin he wore infuriated her. That the others protected themselves, hiding from him behind her.

The Assyrians, her research said, didn't last long as an

empire. They lost their foothold, not through the usual infighting or weak progeny, but because the people they ground under their heels stopped being frightened and fought back. Stole the technology that had enslaved them, and rose up.

She slowed her typing, glancing at the back of his balding head, looking for a seam. A place to slide her letter opener into to create an opening to slip his bones out.

"What's the problem now? Maybe this job is too hard for someone like you." He spun to look at her, a sneering leer on his face. So much scorn in his beady eyes. So much fire burning against her. Lisa didn't respond to him, choosing instead to dive into a gore spattered description of an Assyrian judge stabbing eyes out. Daniel crossed to where she sat and leaned close to her ear.

"What's the matter? Can't take the truth?" He half sat on her desk, folding his arms across his chest and looking down at her. "We all know they hired you to fill the fat girl quota. You don't belong here anymore than a hippo. Oooh, too close to home?"

The others rattled and grumbled, but they didn't so much as peep as he glared around at the others. Damn he had them bulldogged. They smelled the blood in the air. Felt her weakness and knew she'd take the brunt of his attack like a wounded antelope lagging behind the herd.

"You're fat ass, dumb bitch," he whispered in a voice that carried. A voice that cut deep as a razor and stung all the way.

"Fuck you, Daniel," Lisa said, though she wasn't sure where the words came from.

Daniel leaned in, sharp eyeteeth glittering in a wolfish smile. "What'd you say to me, Lisa?"

The words pushed their way out in a rush and her mouth and her muscles worked together, twinning as she wrapped her fingers around the letter opener. Her coworkers kept their heads down, not peering up even as she plunged the letter opener into his stupid beady eye. His mouth fell open, but she pushed so hard that that the tip of the letter opener punched through to his brain. Any snide bullshit, any fat jokes, any complaints about her ineptitude he might have said, died right in his mouth. He gurgled and slumped to the floor. Lisa jerked the opener out with a pop.

She glanced around at the others peering over the tops of their cubicles, watching with wide eyes.

She knew just what she had to do.

The tip of the letter opener slid through his cheeks as she pulled at the new gaping flaps of skin. He squirmed under the pressure of her sawing and ripping. One last pull and his skin came free, scalp and face sliding down his neck. Lisa stood and draped the skin around her neck, face hanging at her throat like a bow.

She turned, stroking the skin of her enemy. Daniel moaned behind his ruined lips, pain laced in the sounds. Lisa smiled at that.

He'd never hurt her again. And the others... They'd see her wearing the skin and they'd know. She'd staked her claim. Conquered the conqueror.

She leaned down and ran her fingers down the seam of Daniel's cuts.

"There, there," she said and pulled him up to sitting, bloodied muscles shining in florescent light. He gibbered and drooled, one eye flashing at her, unblinking without a lid. "I'll be a kinder ruler than you, Daniel."

She turned to them all, her newly conquered people, wanting to be better, more magnanimous than him. Democratic. So, she said, "And you all can wear the skin with me."

THE WAITER AT LE BISTRO
E. D. BURNETTE

The old man was sweating when he entered Le Bistro, bringing an icy blast of February into the restaurant with him.
When he removed his sport coat, I envied his expensive smart
watch and dress shirt, which was too tight and too trendy for
the pleated slacks belted below his potbelly. He looked like a
man eager to fit in, to be more than what he was. At the time,
I remember judging him to be a good tipper and requesting
he be seated in my section; he seemed timid, like the type
of customer who'd apologize for needing extra napkins, then
leave a bigger tip for being too demanding.

And I needed the money. Really needed the money. I'd
just spent my measly savings on a trip to Vegas, trying to
convince myself that my ex-girl and I were better off apart.
I shaved my head and beard, cruised casinos like a baller,
popped some oxy Molly, watched Cirque du Soleil with
Marilyn Monroe by my side, played the guest star with an

adventurous Cleveland couple at the Bellagio, and ended up with the Ace of Spades tattooed on the back of my neck. Can't remember where or how I got that inky souvenir to save my life, but it felt fated. I even convinced my manager to make me a new name tag so I could go by Ace. My old, given name sounded like someone else's bad luck.

But none of it was enough. None of it erased my lovely Raven. Her soft, smooth skin surfing across mine. Her hair, long and velvety black, cascading down the curve of her back. The purr in her throat when she'd speak my name. Her smell still clings fast to me like an addiction.

So when the old man grasped my shirt sleeve and cut off my rundown of the chef's specials, I probably should have shown more empathy, despite the damp spot on my arm from his clammy hand.

"I was supposed to make pan-fried lamb chops with rosemary and garlic for dinner." He spoke slowly and out of one side of his mouth. I couldn't tell if his affectation was a quirk or a consequence of poor health. "Roasted baby carrots. Mint risotto with porcini mushrooms. Lemon and raspberry tart for dessert. I took the day off, went shopping, had it all planned out." He gestured to the brown paper bag, topped with a bouquet of white roses and calla lilies, which sat in the chair facing him.

"Well, we're glad you changed your plans and decided to dine here. Now, the last special of the day is—"

"If I'd said that's what I was making for dinner, young man, wouldn't you have liked to eat that?"

I took out my check book—to discretely shake off his hand—and covered my impatience with a polite smile. "Of course."

"No, no, you're right. I should have taken my wife out for dinner. She even suggested we order the prix fixe á deux here. She was going to have the duck confit and I was going to order the lamb, so we could share." His eyes grew watery. "I miss her."

Curiosity got the best of me. "What happened to your wife, sir?"

"She left me." His bottom lip quivered as tears streamed down his face. "And today's..."

"Valentine's Day." Finally, the anguish on his face made sense. "A day in Hell for those eviscerated by love."

The man's eyes widened. "You understand."

"I do, sir, and I'll see if the kitchen can provide the prix fixe for you at a reduced price. Which apéritif, entrée, and dessert would you prefer then, sir?"

"The steak tartare. The filet mignon, bloody. The Crêpes Suzette. And a bottle of your best Merlot."

I struggled not to gag at the thought of the side salad swimming in a crimson lake on the plate while scribbling on my notepad. "Very good, sir."

As the evening hour grew later, enamored couples swarmed Le Bistro like cockroaches on moldy cheese. They clung together like conjoined twins, heaped endless endearments on one another, and tried to entangle me in their hyper-romanticism.

"Did you know this is our first anniversary?" asked a blonde with too much mascara ringing her bug eyes.

My Raven was married four years when I met her. Said her husband bored her, so I promised I never would. She ghosted me three weeks ago. Three weeks before our first anniversary. I forced a smile. "Congratulations."

"Can we have the back-corner table?" asked a rat-faced man. "For more privacy?" He shared a mischievous chuckle with his mousy date.

That was my Raven's table. She'd eat then linger there until my shift was over. Then we'd go to my apartment and do everything but sleep...I so miss her hair tickling my chest. "Sorry, but that table is already reserved. How about this one over here, with a street view?"

"Psst...Do you think I should propose now, before the escargot comes, or wait until dessert?" asked a twitchy man while his date was in the bathroom.

I really don't give two fucks. In fact, I don't even give a half a fuck. "Do it now and save yourself a couple hundred bucks in case she says no," I advised, then ducked away from the pained shock on his face.

The chattering, the bustle, the overpowering stench of perfumes, colognes, and sex pheromones—all of it was tearing my mind apart, grinding away at my desire to maintain any sense of decorum. I started blanking in the middle of my well-rehearsed recitation of the specials. I asked customers to repeat their orders, and still made some mistakes. I spilled wine in the lap of a woman bedecked in diamonds, who then insisted the manager come out and make me apologize *again* for my incompetence. "Are you okay?" my manager asked me through gritted teeth, and I pretended I was, pretended part of me hadn't died three weeks ago.

My only respite that night was the square of misery surrounding the sweaty old man. He'd undone the top three buttons on his damp shirt, and created a small pile of wet, crumpled napkins next to his plate. I checked on him more than the other customers and teased out his sad story between his bites of tartare.

He called himself Mr. Flom, and he'd spent most of his life pursuing the next great technological wonder, until loneliness finally surmounted his ambition for more wealth. After he spotted his wife waitressing at a benefit gala, he pursued her. Despite their age difference, he thought they'd had a connection. He scaled back his career, financed her entrepreneurial interests, and spoiled her with lavish clothes, jewels, and vacations. Then he discovered the texts to her lover. Heartbroken, but still in love, he gave her a choice: her lover, or her husband.

"I knew when we married that I loved her more," he said. "But I still cannot believe—after everything I've done for her—that she would forsake me. And on today, of all days. I'd been secretly taking cooking classes just so that I could replicate her favorite dish." He gazed woefully at his grocery bag, which had created a small pool of water in its chair.

I shook my head and refilled his glass of Merlot. "I'm so sorry, sir." And I truly was, without any taint of hypocrisy. Mr. Flom didn't deserve to be cuckolded. Not like my Raven's husband, whose arrogant philandering I'd witnessed too many times. "Would you like me to find a place for your bag in one of our refrigerators, so your groceries won't spoil?

Mr. Flom shook his head. "I'll drop everything in the dumpster on my way home."

"I could do that for you now, sir. We have a garbage bin in the alley."

"No, please. I'm not ready yet. Can you please just bring my filet mignon?"

Strangely enough, I thought I understood. "As you wish, sir."

I was a published poet who only ate because of my income as a waiter. I *was* a poet because I haven't been able to string together as much as a lune since I lost my Raven. Before her, I could find inspiration in the soap bubbles lingering in the sink. When she loved me, my creativity mushroomed even more, and sometimes my pen could barely keep up with my own thoughts. She gave me pure, incandescent happiness, and made all the best parts of me better. I had never felt like that before and, certainly, will never feel that way again. Which is why I will never forgive her despicable husband,

Michael Celino, for taking my Raven from me.

I realize how hypocritical I must sound but trust me. Michael is the other man. Not me.

He strutted into Le Bistro that night with a Jessica Rabbit redhead on his arm, just as I emerged from the kitchen. Trays of food teetered in my hands and, of course, he stopped squarely in my path. I tried to circumvent him, but whichever side I moved to, so did he. On purpose. As my arms began to tremble, he laughed, drawing attention from everywhere.

"I just can't seem to get out of your way, can I?" Michael said.

"We all have our flaws," I replied.

"So true. And so sad when we can't rise above them. Maybe you should write a poem about that. You know, milk your personal experience. Things with heart always sell, right?" He laughed as if that were actually funny.

"I'm already working on something more profound, but thanks." I hated that my bravado rang false to my own ears. I tried to go around him, but he mirrored me. Again. The drinks on my tray sloshed dangerously, and as I struggled to keep them steady, Syrah dribbled over the rim of a glass. My temper flared. "Speaking of flaws...how's PosturePro doing?"

He flinched so slightly that the confidence in his next words was almost believable. "Like a rockstar. My most prescient startup yet. Never expected a vibrating belt to help you sit up straighter could be such a gamechanger. You should apply to be an assembler there. From what I hear, it'd pay a lot more than poetry and waiting tables."

"How generous of you," I said with oil-slick smoothness. "So, the rumors about the burns from PosturePro's belt aren't true then? Because that would be a disaster, wouldn't it?"

There really weren't any rumors until that moment, not until my loud words whipped heads around and stirred the whispers of curious, gossipy patrons. I had been in the habit of keeping Raven's confidence and snickering at her husband's failings with her in private—before she disappeared from my life. Before she left me bereft of all happiness. For a wasteland of human decency. For *him*.

His face flamed, and his date dropped his arm as though he might detonate. Feeling smug, I took advantage of his stupefaction to finally circumvent him. Or so I thought.

Before I could walk away and resume my server duties, he pressed a cold, calloused finger to the back of my neck, right on top of my Ace of Spades tattoo. His finger felt wet with hateful spit.

A nasty shiver went through me, like a snake slithering under the surface of my skin. And the food balanced on my barely steady hands crashed to the floor.

Perhaps I should have pointed out what he'd done then and there, instead of allowing him to escape under the guise of the-customer-is-always-right. Perhaps I shouldn't have been afraid of making a scene with the techie prince and risking my employment even further. But what exactly had he done to me, except touch my neck? Even if he had licked his finger beforehand, I hadn't seen him do it and maybe I only imagined the vile wetness. I couldn't explain the violence of my reaction, not even to myself. The whole episode made me feel weak. So, I decided to cover my weakness with a lie of clumsiness.

After cleaning the mess, washing my neck, and enduring a painful teardown by my manager in the kitchen, I went to each of my affected tables and apologized for delaying their meal. Most of my customers were understandably miffed yet polite. But Mr. Flom saw the cracks in my façade.

"Who made you drop the food?" he asked.

"No one, sir. Everyone has days when gravity opposes them."

"Gravity drags us down all the time, but we still stand tall. It is other people who destroy us and—"

His gaze wandered past me, and as I looked around to see what had caught his attention, I spotted Michael Celino and Jessica Rabbit sitting at a table. In my section.

I should have known then that the heavens were preparing to shit on me.

Michael smiled and waved, and when I turned around (fighting like mad not to give him the finger), Mr. Flom was waving back. Yet the tightness of his jaw suggested he'd rather eat vomit-soaked glass.

"Is something wrong, sir?"

"No...yes..." Mr. Flom's cheeks swelled as if the words were fighting to be free. "Michael and I sit on the same board of directors, and we rarely agree on anything. Once he called me 'out of touch', so I called him 'an irrelevant neophyte'. On top of that...I suspect my wife is—I mean, was—having an affair with that man." He let out a heavy sigh, and tears rimmed his eyes. "An affair's only an affair if the husband doesn't know, right?"

I shook my head, imagining my poor, poor Raven forced to smile at Mr. Flom's wife and endure Michael's boundless whoredom. "I wish I could say I was surprised, sir, but the truth is I've seen evidence of Mr. Celino's philandering firsthand. He brings both his wife and his mistresses here, and never bothers taking off his wedding ring."

"Very unscrupulous."

"Completely. I wish I knew why any woman would put up with someone like Mr. Celino. Is money truly capable of replacing love?"

"You take his behavior very personally."

I refilled his wine glass while considering how transparent I should be. He was my customer, after all, and why should I risk the size of my tip? But his honesty proved contagious.

"Mr. Celino's wife often ate here when he was out of town. She confided in me. So, I can see his sins clearly through her eyes."

"You talk as if she's stopped coming here."

I simply nodded so that I could swallow the painful lump in my throat.

"You were in love with her, weren't you?"

Again, I could only nod. Love was such an inadequate word. And, it seemed, all the love I possessed was inadequate.

"It might amuse you to hear my wife's nickname for him. 'H&H'. That's how he's listed in her phone contacts. Stands for Heaven and Hell. Only when I saw the name 'Michael' buried in the body of one of the texts did I know for sure it was him." When I frowned, he added, "Because Celino means angel or sky in Italian. Like heaven."

Raven used to call me Michael when we first met, when I was only her waiter. After we became lovers, I pleaded with her to at least call me Angelo, my middle name, since I hated sharing the same first name as her husband. When she would forget this, she insisted it was because she always called her husband Mike, not Michael. Part of me never fully believed her and worried she might see me as no better, no different, than her husband.

My chest tightened; it seemed my insecurities rang true. "Would you like me to ask him to leave on your behalf?" And on mine as well, I thought.

"No," he replied without hesitation. "I came here tonight for the very purpose of confronting my wife's infidelity and making my own peace with it. Please send Michael a bottle of wine from me."

"As you wish," I grumbled. "How much money would like to waste on Mr. Celino?"

"Actually, the bottle is in my grocery bag."

When I started to retrieve it, he practically hissed, "No!"

Then he jumped up and pulled out a very rare and expensive bottle of French Pinot Noir, which my Raven had brought to Le Bistro on more than one occasion. To say my mind devolved at that moment would be both an understatement and an exaggeration; although I was aware of the present happenings, I also became a prisoner of the past, frozen to the faux rustic tile upon which I stood. For the last time my Raven had brought that Pinot to Le Bistro was the last time I saw her, touched her, wrapped her legs around me, buried my face in her long dark hair. We made urgent love behind the building on my break, and afterwards I begged her to spend the night with me. "Your scent is fading from my bed," I'd pleaded. But all she said was, "I can't, Michael. I can't."

At the time, I thought her face was full of longing for me and consequential sadness. But I could have mistaken longing for fear at having been found out. When she used my given name, perhaps I should have questioned that red flag. Just as I should have asked Mr. Flom why his bottle of Pinot Noir was already uncorked.

But, as I said, the past had imprisoned me—and, I now confess, my present jealousy corrupted me. So I watched Mr. Flom small-talk and chuckle and pour his peace offering into Mr. Celino's and Jessica Rabbit's glasses like an unconscionable quadriplegic. I watched Mr. Celino and his date toast with their gift, then drink it heartily. Only when their eyes bulged and their mouths frothed did I lose my paralysis and fully register Mr. Flom sniffling and whispering, "I loved my wife...I loved my Raven..."

That's when something compelled me to look in his grocery bag. When I truly knew Hell. When I found, buried beneath the white roses and calla lilies, a lifeless mass of bloody, black hair.

SWALLOWED WORDS
JANELLE EVANS

Mrs. Cardom is an impeccably dressed, dainty sixty year old whose waistline hasn't changed since her sixteenth birthday. This is a widely known fact, mostly because she tells it to everyone she meets. It is not her only vanity, but it is certainly one that she attends to with excruciating vigilance. Witness her choice of an undressed salad while dining at one of Manhattan's finest French restaurants.

"This is my first meal of the day. You will not spoil it." Mrs. Cardom sips water from a crystal goblet.

Across from her sits Agata, the eldest of Mrs. Cardom's five children. Agata has wisely chosen to order the soupe à l'oignon. The rich broth and fragrant cheese produce an enticing aroma. Not that you'd know this from the expression on her face, or the mulish way that she pokes at the food without ever tasting it.

"Let me help you." Mrs. Cardom scoops the cheese from

the top of the soup with exquisite precision, leaving behind only the crust that has baked onto the sides of the bowl.

"How true to form of you, to take away the best part."

"There's still plenty of fat in there for you to enjoy. I've only removed the solid portion. No doubt your doctor and your hips are thankful."

This is clearly a well-worn territory for mother and daughter, which explains the look of surprise on Mrs. Cardom's face when Agata doesn't respond to the salvo.

"It should've been a yellow dress, with daisies or buttercups. Sylvie loved anything yellow." Agata laughs softly. The sound is musical, enchanting. What you'd expect from classically trained opera singer. Her face is tender, wistful. "Do you remember when she said she wanted jaundice, so that her skin could be yellow?"

"My poor sweet girl." Mrs. Cardom sniffs, forks up a leaf of dry spring greens. She chews the single leaf in perfect silence. "Such a good girl."

The mild words wash the vulnerability from Agata's face.

"Do you know that the neighbors never heard her scream? Not even once." Agata's silver spoon clinks against the sides and bottom of the china dish. Around and round the spoon goes, tink-tink-tink, calling for attention.

"Mommy's good little quiet girl." Mrs. Cardom glares at Agata, spears another leaf from the salad plate. "Not like the rest of you, always needing to be reminded that our home was not a barnyard."

"Nope, never needed a reminder. But you gave them to her anyway, didn't you? She got her share, earned or not."

"She was my little mouse." The older woman dabs her eyes with her linen napkin, continues having the conversation that she's chosen to have, and not the conversation that her daughter wants to have. "I think they did a wonderful job on the tombstone, don't you? The ruffles on the mouse princess' tutu have real sense of movement to them."

"She always hated that nickname. We all did. That's why we called her bunny. That, and the way she'd scream when she was getting her reminders."

"Mouse never needed reminding." Mrs. Cardom leans forward, pretends that she's truly observing her daughter. "Of course. High as always. Even at your baby sister's funeral."

"Of course I am. How else could I stand to spend a whole afternoon with you?" Her beautiful laugh does nothing to soften the harsh words.

"You didn't have to come. We could've said our goodbyes without you and the taint of the filthy things that you do to get your drugs." The sound of her own righteous rhetoric adds savor to her meal, and the next mouthful of salad consists of a whole three leaves.

"We? Look around you, mother. You have four living children, and exactly one of them showed up today. Why do you think that is?"

"Because my other children hold positions of responsibility and trust. They are busy with careers of import and matter. You are an unemployed bum, whose brother bought her a plane ticket."

"I'm here because I pulled the shortest straw. And my brother bought my ticket and my drugs, because he felt sorry for me when I lost."

"If this is such an odious duty, why don't you just go?" Mrs. Cardom grips the handle of her fork, the tines pointed toward Agata like so many tiny spears.

"And let yours be the last face above Bunny's open grave? Not on your life." She pulls an ornate compact from her purse, takes out a pill and holds it up to the light. She stares her mother in the eye, then dry-swallows the pill.

"Disgusting." Mrs. Cardom throws her napkin for emphasis. A nearby waiter snatches it up midflight. Money buys so much overlooked magic. "I'm going to the powder room. You may excuse yourself while I'm away."

Agata watches her mother's departure, a smile slowly growing on her face. She's thinking that her uptight, abusive, bitch of a mother has never once been out of control. She's thinking it might be nice to see that, if only once in her lifetime.

When the runner places their main courses on the table, a brilliant idea occurs to her. Making sure that no one's looking, she takes a baggie out of her purse and crumbles a few mushrooms into her mother's cassoulet.

"Good thing you don't take cheese." Agata snickers as she stirs the famous hallucinogen into Mrs. Cardom's meal.

In her mind and blood, the process is slow and delicious. It spreads out and lingers, like taffy pulled on a warm summer day. Agata motions with her hand and the napkin-catching waiter takes the dirty spoon and replaces it with a clean one.

"Still here?" Mrs. Cardom positions herself so that the waiter can easily push her chair forward as she sits down. It could be the sertraline that she'd just taken, but Agata is almost certain that the waiter had given her a conspirator's wink as he'd pushed her mother's chair in.

"That's what you said to me the night I graduated High School. To all of us. Even Bunny. Why did you have so many children, when you hated us all so very much?"

"I refuse to converse with you when you are under the influence of illicit substances." Nose slightly in the air, Mrs. Cardom eats her first spoonful of the cassoulet.

"High, mother, you could've just said high. Like everyone else."

"That is your problem. You wish to be like everyone else. The word for that is common. A synonym is cheap." More cassoulet, because hurling insults builds up an appetite.

"Common isn't a synonym for cheap. It means widely

available, and some things are supposed to be that way. Like a mother's love."

"Like anything of merit, love should be earned." She lifts the spoon toward her mouth, frowns, holds it at arm's length.

"Is there a concern, Madame?" The miraculous, napkin-catching waiter bends solicitously toward Mrs. Cardom.

"No, not at all." She forces the bite of food into her mouth. It's an effort, attested to by the faint sheen of perspiration on her brow. She chews, and chews, but swallowing is beyond her. "Excuse," little particles of food spray from her mouth.

"That's disgusting, mother. You should go to the powder room."

If she hadn't been in such distress, Mrs. Cardom would've given Agata a verbal lashing for daring to give her instructions. As she hurries to the ladies' room, she plans what she'll say when she returns.

But all laid plans, of mice and men, rarely come to fruition. Which is why it is a very silent Mrs. Cardom who rides home in the limousine with Agata. Nonverbal, however, doesn't mean uncommunicative, and Mrs. Cardom's arms, legs, hands, and even her torso, insist on moving about and performing a wholly improvised dance interpretation of her inner rage.

"Dance, Mommy, dance!" Agata claps in time to her mother's gyrations. "Let it loose, woman."

Mrs. Cardom continues to twist and turn, her face white and contorted. She's in pain from the constant motion but unable to stop.

"I did this to you. Yes, I did." Her giggles fill the rear of the car. The driver opens the door, allowing her merriment to trip out into the night sky. "You may go, Herbert."

"Thank you, Ms. Agata." He tips his hat and walks away. There's relief in his stride, even a touch of satisfaction. He'd been watching the two ladies on the camera in the front of the vehicle, and enjoying every minute of Mrs. Cardom's discomfort. Her children are not the only people subject to her cruelty.

"Come along, Mommy. Let's get you to bed." She pulls the older woman easily from the car. "Good thing you're still my double digits girl."

Upstairs, in Mrs. Cardom's massive bathroom, Agata starts a hot bath. The tub has a very unique design, with the bottom of the tub having a lower side than the top, making it easier for an elderly to step in and out, and a dip in the middle, so that a person sitting inside can still have a very full bath. She tests the water temperature, then adds a generous helping of magnesium enriched sea salts.

"Don't be wasteful with my belongings." Mrs. Cardom clings to the sink vanity. Her body movements are still beyond her control, but she can speak again.

"The magnesium will stop you from having cramps. But you're right, anything that eases your pain is waste." She pulls the stopper and the water begins to drain.

"Stupid cow." Mrs. Cardom lunges toward Agata, slips and falls to her knees. She's just spry enough to catch herself on the side of the tub, preventing a nasty bump on the head. She pants, slumped halfway into the tub. "Stop it before it all drains away."

"Make up your mind, Miss Meanie." Agata plugs the tub again, turns the water back on. Settles on the edge of the tub beside her mother. She pats the woman's hair gently, a softness in keeping with childlike inflection that her voice has taken on. "That's what we called you, Miss Meanie. Always yelling at us for silence. Hitting us for not being silent enough. Horrible, horrible Miss Meanie."

The water fills the tilted tub efficiently. There's no overfill drain on the walk-in tub, because Mrs. Cardom enjoys a deep bath, one with enough water to cover her up to her neck. It's not that high yet. Right now, it barely covers her elbows. This is the deep end of the tub.

"You were all rotten, ungrateful brats. I married, over and over again. Just to keep a roof over your heads, and food in your mouth. All of those sweaty, hairy, disgusting nights. A little quiet was not too much to ask."

"Babies aren't quiet, Mommy."

"They can be trained to be quiet. The water is too warm." It rises steadily, covers her elbows. "Did you hear me? It is too warm."

"You need the warmth."

Mrs. Cardom whimpers, then hurls a spectacular amount of the night's meal into the bathwater.

"Whew." Agata fans the air in front of her face. "Smells like somebody was drinking on an empty stomach."

The vile water rises ever higher. Bits of her stomach's putrid jetsam begin to stick to her chest and upper arms. Mrs. Cardom squirms, trying to slide way from the bath. She only succeeds in sliding downward. Now her entire torso rests in the foot portion of the tub.

Thanks to the unique design that we were discussing, this portion of the tub is still empty. The upper portion, deep portion, which is a deep U-shaped area, designed to cup the bather from buttocks to neck, is still filling. Soon it will be high enough to crest the other side of the U, and begin to spill downward. The downward flow fills the lower portion of the tub, and you can turn the water off, just as soon as there's enough to cover your feet and knees. Money buys so many undreamt of levels of comfort.

"Help me up." Mrs. Cardom has not yet realized the predicament that she's in.

"I read the police report." Agata remains perched on the high end of the tub. She stares down at the lap of her skirt. With the tip of her finger, she outlines the shape of a bunny face, triangle nose, whiskers and all.

"Liar. It hasn't been released because they're still hunting for that animal."

"Did so. That nice detective sneaked me a copy. And do you know what? She didn't have any defensive wounds. Not a single one."

The first trickle of overflow splashes against Mrs. Cardom. Semi-digested salad leaves stick to her face. She wriggles until she's almost sideways in the water. "Turn the water off."

"No screaming. No fighting. Just dying."

"The water." She had to tilt her head slightly backward to avoid drinking her own sick. And even then, she'd only gained a precious inch of reprieve.

"He had her for over four hours. Cutting her, raping her, torturing her." Agata stands, slowly, dreamily, begins to walk toward her mother. The water is just beneath Mrs. Cardom's nose when her daughter kneels down beside her. "And just like you taught her, she didn't scream, she didn't fight. She didn't even try to run. She was a good little mouse."

"Agata, please." She chokes and splutters on mouthful of the nasty water. Her body flops and twitches, still galvanized by the cassoulet's secret ingredient. The movement slides her further into the tub. Her perfectly coiffed hair becomes soaked and heavy, long hanks swirling about like fronds until they find their way home, to wrap themselves around their mistress's neck. Mrs. Cardom thrashes and chokes, gurgles, vomits up some of the water that she's inhaled and is forced to choke down even more.

Agata kneels beside the older woman, she watches until the last bubble has formed and popped.

THE PROPHET
JAMILLA VANDYKE-BAILEY

She watched, entranced, as the windshield wipers slid back and forth, clearing away the raindrops.

"Daddy?"
"Yes?"
"What's wrong with Mumma. Is she sleeping?"

He looked into the backseat; her face was bright, brown, and plain. He smiled and returned his eyes to the road.

"Mumma wasn't feeling well, Baby, so she took some medicine to help her feel better."
"Oh."

He waited patiently, as she thought of another question to ask.

"Wait, Daddy?"

"Yes?"

"Where are we going? It's raining."

Her eyes started following the wipers. *mmph. mmph. mmph. mmph.*

"Well, I can't tell you. It's a surprise."

"Wow"

She said *wow* the way that kids do; excited and confused all at once.

"Yes, Baby. It's a big surprise."

Terrance gripped the steering wheel, frustrated with himself for lying. He didn't like lying to anyone, let alone his own flesh and blood. Leviticus 19:11 says: *Do not steal. Do not lie. Do not deceive one another.* But, he figured, no one is perfect but the Lord.

She drummed her fingertips on the window to mimic the beat of the wipers. *mmph. mmph. mmph. mmph.* With the rain, falling on the car softly, and the tap-tap-tapping on the back-seat window, he felt the weight of his head start to slip.

"Baby, can you stop? I can't focus on the road with all that tapping."

"Okay, Daddy."

But a minute later she was tapping again, much softer, as if he wouldn't be able to hear it. Terrence couldn't take his eyes off the road, it was getting harder to see. He glanced over at his wife, slumped in the passenger's seat in a sleep so deep,

Baby's screaming probably wouldn't cut through it.

Terrance started to hum.

"Daddy? Whatcha humming?"

He looked into the rearview mirror for a moment and watched her mindlessly tapping the window again and again.

"Guess. I'll give you a hint."
"Okay, go"
"It's the song I've been playing so much lately."
"The one Mumma said she's tired of hearing?"

He looked at his sleeping wife, with love.

"Yeah, that one."
"Oh! I like it, can I sing it too?"

They began to sing as he continued to thrust the car down the highway.

Better get ready for judgment
You better get ready for judgment morning
You better get ready for judgment
My God is coming down

Better get ready for judgment
For God is coming down
The cloud will bear His horses
Where men begin to frowned

She said, "frowned," instead of "frown." Strangely, it irritated him a little; but at the same time, he felt the need to laugh. He couldn't believe that she knew all the lyrics, but then again he had been playing it incessantly morning, day, and night.

He wasn't really familiar with the song, but one night, when he was still, God spoke to him. He said the lyrics, so slow and so soft and so clear, that Terrence wondered if he was hallucinating the whole thing. The next morning, he hummed the song while fixing himself a pot of coffee.

"I remember that old song; Judgment by Sister Mary Nelson,"

Marsha said as she kissed him on the cheek.

"Whenever me and John-John were bad, Ma used to make us sing it until Daddy came home. I still remember the bruises he would put on me back then"

"Proverbs 13:24 states, *He who spares the rod, hates his son. But he who loves him disciplines him diligently*"

"Say that to John-John's broken pinky toe, that never healed quite right."

> *Better get ready for judgment*
> *You better get ready for judgment morning*
> *You better get ready for judgment*
> *My God is coming down*
>
> *Better put on your morning garment*
> *And get your staff in your hand*
> *For Jesus coming that morning*
> *He's coming unaware to man*

Before he left the house that morning, Terrence had the song downloaded to his phone. And by the time he made it into the office, he had listened to the song at least twenty times, leaving no time for him to listen to any of his usual gospel tracks. After a while, Terrence got the words and cadence memorized so well, that he no longer needed to sing along with his phone. When he was at home, or on the road, he would sing the song with confidence, slow, soft, and clear. Or, he would hum it.

Terrence had to admit, he had become obsessed with the song, but he figured that God put it on his spirit and his mind for a reason; and it was his responsibility to figure out why.

With his mind back in the car he could hear the tap tap tapping again. Snapping his head to the backseat he said,

"I thought I told you to stop that tapping."

But it was no use, when Baby had the spirit, she had the spirit and no one could get through to her but God.

> Better get ready for judgment
> You better get ready for judgment morning
> You better get ready for judgment
> My God is coming down
>
> Well, all you hippopotamuses
> You wasting your time away
> My God's calling for workmens
> And you had better obey

Yes, obey. Obey God. At all costs. Like Abraham was willing to do. Terrence had wanted to obey God since he was a kid, when his mother would drag him behind her to church five nights out of the week. Other kids would sit in the back, mad; but Terrence would sing along, clapping his hands, thinking about God.

It's true that Terrence lost his footing when he got a little older and went to college. But when the darkness started walking its way deeper into his mind, he found himself under the hands of his mother who called on God to heal his spirit. She called on God to bring light into Terrence. His mother said it was just the devil trying to weasel his way into God's plans. Marsha said that WebMD called it schizophrenia.

Against his mother's wishes, he started taking meds. And the darkness went away. And God went away.

> *Better get ready for judgment*
> *You better get ready for judgment morning*
> *You better get ready for judgment*
> *My God is coming down*
>
> *The gamblers, the drunkards, the liars*
> *And the adulterers, too*
> *Well, all these false pretenders*
> *And all them hippopotamuses too*

Back in the car, he pushed the car faster and said,

> "It's hypocrites not hippopotamuses"

But Baby was in the Spirit. Deep, deep in the spirit.

It was the Spirit that came to him a month or two ago. At first, he didn't know what it was, it had been years since the darkness and God. He was swishing the mouthwash back and forth, above and beneath his tongue, counting to himself, when he heard this voice, moving throughout him tell him to *Spit*. So he did. It told him to *Take out the pill bottles* and he grabbed the ones with his names on them. *Flush them.* The voice, the spirit, then ordered him through replacing the pills, the devil pills, with Advil.

As the days began to blur, the Spirit let in the darkness, but he also let in God. Terrence didn't realize how much he missed God, but he knew he had to keep it from Marsha, or else she would make him go back there; back to a time without God.

He would talk to God at night. But lately, God has been wanting to talk during the day too. He wanted to show him things. He wanted to show Terrence the blessings of his life, like a wife who loved him, and appreciated the fact that he made her coffee in the morning. *A wife who would heed.* Terrence was also blessed with Baby. Baby who was so full of the spirit, herself.

> *Better get ready for judgment*
> *You better get ready for judgment morning*
> *You better get ready for judgment*
> *My God is coming down*
>
> *When Jesus get tired pleading*
> *And He won't pleads no more*
> *He'll call the world together*
> *He'll call the young and old*

It was a calling, wasn't it. All of this. A calling. A sign, a calling. A judgment. A calling to action with them together.

Back to the car, Terrence told Baby to sing louder. She closed her eyes so tight, she never saw the trees running.

Better get ready for the judgment.
You better get ready for judgment morning
You better get ready for judgment
My God is coming down!

Terrence, leaning forward with a smile and love, shouted backwards over her wailing,

"GET READY, BABY!"

She sang as loud as possible,

BETTER GET READY FOR JUDGMENT. YOU BETTERGETREADYFORJUDGMENTMORNING YOU BETTER GET READY—

She flung her eyes open at the sound of the car thudding, and saw her father's face in full grin as the ocean reached up to meet the windshield. He caught the ghost and said,

"Get ready to meet GOD!"

MOMMA
KACIE PROLOGO

Neither of the Nickels boys seemed bothered when the first shot went wild over their heads. Could be they weren't really all that surprised. Wasn't just but the two of us lounging on the porch under the eaves of the house, Momma in her rocker tapping her foot against the pine deck boards, both of us sipping coffee from a couple cracked earth mugs. Some of that cold stove brew, black and thick with no milk to cut through it, slipped over the silver hairs on Momma's upper lip, staining them back to the darker brown of her youth.

"Suppose this means Dennis ain't got 'round to puttin' up them fences yet," Momma said, cocking the Savage 110 she kept in the mud room next to our winter hats and scarves.

"Suppose it does," I said.

For a time, we watched as the brothers picked their way over the deadfall at the edge of the yard, Noland Nickels kicking at hillocks of mushrooms as they passed into the damp of the low field While Garret, older than Noland by no more than a year but already bigger than most of the teenagers that ran the alleys on the East end of town, dragged after his brother like a belt beat dog, Momma slid another bullet from the front pocket of her housecoat. Thirty – ought – sixes didn't come cheap as they used to, but Momma kept herself a full box in the cupboard next to the sugar bowl just the same.

"Don't think I don't see you," Momma called. "Had eyes on you boys even before ya'll crossed over from the woods."

Laughing, Noland pulled back the breech on a bastardly looking Red Ryder while Noland fired toward the house, something I heard more than saw, but then the tin pan sound of a half-dozen BBs crashing against aluminum siding hasn't changed much since my own boyhood days. Momma used the noise to aim. Her next shot kicked up a plume of dirt right in front of the Noland's sneakered feet, a crack shot for a woman with first signs of arthritis twisting her fingers.

In her prime, Momma would've known those boys were headed for our property before they'd even decided for themselves, would've had their names wrapped around her tongue. Used to be kids came looking for Momma either because friends dared them to or because their own mommas let it slip that the ramshackle ranch at the end of Williford Lane was the home of a woman who read futures in farm dirt and spun fortunes from junk. Rumor was Momma knew how to make squash sprout out of the valley clay and how to make tax audits disappear. She knew which of a man's cattle was gonna wind up with its guts all busted out on the side of the highway just by giving the dumb beasts a once over, could even make a close guess as to how many black flies would come buzzing for the entrails. Wasn't a farmer's wife in three counties hadn't hauled themselves through Momma's door looking for salves and creams that stank of the dredges of our garden.

Wasn't but a bunch of cheap tricks bought for a song by any idiot willing to open up their wallets. Momma saved her best work for the desperate and the lonely, chopping red clover and boiling milk thistle while women who couldn't catch pregnant hung their heads over her dining room table.

"Slip some a' this in yer' man's beer," Momma would say, "an' I bet he'll have enough heft in his pecker to fill out yer' belly with twins."

Momma would laugh then, a sound that set the women to shivering.

Still, no one said the word *witch*, not then.

Out in the weeds that used to be Momma's flowerbeds, about sixty yards from the last tree and to the far right,

, parasol wads of white flesh flinging out into the night. Whole place would run to rot if I didn't bust my hump keeping the mildew and moss from hanging off our asses. Still, wouldn't be nothing but ringless honeys and bullfrogs to pick through if the rain didn't let up.

Anymore, the damp cramped Momma's bones up so she had to shuffle from her Lazy-Boy to the rocker on the porch. Just to get going in the morning, I had to wrap Momma's hands around her coffee cup so the warmth of it relaxed , and the carpet around her rocking chair stank of the peppered burns from where she overshot the ashtray with her cigarettes. Just last year Momma's eyes started milking over, a film of white fogging over the gunmetal grey of her iris. Wasn't much to be done about it. Every night Momma brewed herself up a healing tea, saffron and garlic mixed through with agrimony to save what sight she had. Every night she went to bed with an oven-heated towel draped across her face for circulation. Doc Halloran who ran the Urgent Care over on Belmont promised Momma she'd be blind by Christmas.

"Price of living," Halloran told her, wiping his own glasses against the sleeve of his shirt. "Haven't found a thing yet that fixes aging."

"Brats," Momma said. "World ain't nothin' but brats anymore."

Everett Stadler sparked the first match, running his mouth that the ol' hag must've had a hand in the disappearance of his brood of slack-jawed daughters. Didn't help that Momma managed to bring in more than her fair share of parsnips and beat root when Everett didn't have nothing to his name but the boils on his backside.

"Poor girls," Everett would say once he got in on the brandy down at the See Horse Inn. "They must've gone off to play an' got themselves turned around. Bet they stumbled out of the corn right into that bitch's back yard."

Most folks rolled their eyes and sipped their beers. Couldn't trust Everett any farther than his credit line, but a man tells the same story, tells it over and over as the months ticked by, eventually it doesn't seem so much like a story anymore.

By the time the state came in to repave all the off ramps east of the Pine Wood river, half the damn town swore up and down they'd seen Momma lining the Stadler girls face down in her garden, each of them dressed for Sunday with a different colored ribbon holding the hair off the napes of their necks and one of Momma's hill folk symbols scratched into the tops of their spines, a pert and perfect sacrifice.

Personally, I only seen the sisters twice myself: once in the parking lot of Schneider's Mill where their daddy liked to keep everyone else waiting while he haggled with Anna-Lee Schneider over the price of chicken feed. From a distance, they looked like a row of nesting dolls, each one a painted copy of the next oldest on down to Margret Stadler, the first-born daughter. Christ but she was the prettiest little thing.

"Even a dumbass like Everett could fetch up a good dowry for the likes a' her," Momma would say. "Could gather up all the farmer's sons for six counties and have us a grand ol' auction."

She'd wrung the neck of one of our spring chickens as she said it but the smile that pulled the cracked flat of Momma's lips across her teeth never reached up to the fading blue of her one good eye. Story was that Momma went to daddy, a knock-kneed miller's son, for just enough rough-cut lumber to repair her poppa's barn, and they were married that same day. Momma wore the clothe she'd been sent out of her family house in – a stitched to fit dress made from bits of her poppa's old work shirts and a gummy pair of rain boots.

Daddy taken her on their wedding night against the cold wood stove near his workbench. He socked her one when she wouldn't stop crying and punched her again when some of the blood from her nose splashed on his last good pair of jeans. In the time before they'd moved away from the mill to the wide tract of land that would become Momma's farm, she'd lost three babies to daddy's fists.

"Can't go lookin' to put reason to it," Momma said. "Some men 're just born with a gut full of mean."

Wasn't two months into their first real season on the farm when Momma planted daddy in the ground. I don't know that anyone came asking after him. I don't know why anyone would. It was three years of thaw and frost, three years after Momma delivered her only living child into the muck of her fresh tilled garden, before someone took up the task of checking on the miller's son and his fresh new wife. By then, only poppa's bones were left and even then the crows and coyotes had carried off their fair share.

The second time I saw the Stadlers they were tossing rocks at Ugly Ricky, Momma's half-tame tabby. He'd come out of the hills the same year that daddy died, top lip snarled over the teeth jutting out from his jaw, twin chunks missing from either side of his right ear. Never was a feral cat so rangy. Thing stalked around the farm flashing its claws at anything that got too close.

"Ain't he such a good boy," she would say, fingers ghosting over the mange on Ricky's back. "A good ol' boy just for me."

One of those girls, and I've still half a mind that it must've been Margret, fired a piece of flint sharpened river stone at Ricky's narrow flanks, peeling back a piece of muscle and mangy fur. The girls jumped around, congratulating themselves as the cat slunk away to lick its wound. Their straw-colored curls looked almost silver in the moonlight.

"They don't mean nothin' by it," I said, but Momma just looked out into the dark, her eyes reflecting the light of the harvest moon.

Eventually, they found Margret's bones in a culvert near the strip mines, the smooth curve of her skull poking up from a tangle of dandelions and McDonald's wrappers. Of Margret's sisters, the smaller Stadlers who'd come one after the other even after Everett lost his ability to cultivate just about everything else, there weren't even scraps.

Sheriff Braddon snooped around Momma's for a bit, losing the shine of his shoes in the dust of our dooryard. "Best if you lay low for a while," he'd said, running his hands through the Vitalis slick of his hair. "We don't wanna go gettin' people all riled up."

Would've been his right to cuff her, to throw her in the back of his cruiser – a 94 Toyota Corolla donated by the Woman's league after Braddon's old car wound up at the bottom of Stirling Lake. Instead, he backed his car down the drive, headlight's bobbing across the yard and the woods. So far as I know, the sheriff never came back. Whole town figured he'd gone sweet on Momma.

Guess that's about when the farm wives stopped coming

with their ailments and the boys from Matlin Ave. started creeping in with more stones hidden in their pockets and BB guns slung over their shoulders. Once, the ladies from the First Friends Church came to beg for the Stadler girls' immortal souls.

"There won't be no rest for em' as long as they ain't buried right," the ladies said.

Momma just rolled her rheumy eyes.

Come that same winter, we got it on good word that Everett started spending most of his nights with the soft mushroom of his gut flush against the scratch and peel bar at the Sea Horse Inn. He'd slap down a hundred-dollar bill, it's edges still crisp from the bank envelope tucked in his back pocket and wouldn't get up from his stool until he'd drank the whole thing down.

"Goddamn growing season boys," Everett said, his arm slung around a bleach fried blond, one hand alternating between the loose skin of her right breast and the hemline of her mini skirt. It should be said that Mrs. Stadler lived and died with a head of dark hair pulled to a tight bun at the base of her neck.

Talk ran that Everett finally found himself pulling more black than red in his bank accounts after the first harvest his farm had seen in over ten years. Must've been that Marshall Larson, who took over the tending of The Sea Horse after his own bar burned to the ground, saw the greasy well-fed look on Mr. Stadler's face and knew he'd traded up for something.

Time was Marshall had a sister of his own, a redhead who took after their mother in that she'd beat up every boy at Morgan Elementary and could slam down a stack of flap jacks tall enough to feed Marshall, his daddy, and both hired farm hands. Like Everett, Marshall's daddy fought tooth and nail for a scraggle of field fit enough to even sprout cow corn but kept on like any man with a world of trouble on his back.

After another dry summer, he sent Marshall's spitfire sister across the way to Momma's, hoping the girl would come back with magic enough to save them. Trouble was, she never came back. Marshall begged his daddy to call the sheriff. Came close to picking up the phone himself a few times, but then the fields started growing in tall and thick. Marshall's daddy got the bank off their ass and life went on a little easier with fewer mouths to feed.

Marshall never did bother with any of the suspicious notions rotting out the corners of his mind. Could be he didn't consider it in his best interest to go getting all mixed up in what wasn't really his business. Could be that Everett started paying on his bar tab, a real miracle. Wasn't really much left in the world to surprise Momma.

The boys scuffled to a stop, and their eyes must've caught the burning tip of Momma's cigarette from across the last of our open field. If either Garrett or Noland suspected the tremor in Momma's hands or saw her struggling against the weight of her own gun, then neither of them seemed to think it enough to gamble an escape on.

I can't say for sure Momma really meant to shoot those boys. A lifetime of mean living puts a person on edge. Push hard enough and they start running on the kind of instincts that bloody the teeth of most animals. I might've stopped Momma if I had any guts about me, I might've made to save those boys, but Momma had kept all the guts in the family to herself, hording all the brave and all the mean too. Maybe Garrett sensed that truth between me and Momma. He sat down in the dirt and the chicken scratch and tried not to cry.

"My mom says you're not really a witch," Garrett called, pulling his legs to his chest, scraped knees and bent elbows spilling out into the chilled October air. He bit down on his bottom lip, a gesture that could only belong to a kid whose mind was just starting to get too big for its age. "Mom says there ain't no such thing," he yelled.

"Sounds like a smart woman," Momma said. "Smart women usually raise smart boys."

Noland curled his lip like a struck dog. "Everyone knows you do the devil's work," he shouted. "That's what poppa says. Everyone knows yer' goin' to hell."

"Boy," Momma said. She pulled another cigarette out of a softening pack with the blunt ends of her teeth. Her other hand, still cradling most of the rifle against her belly, fiddled with the junction switch she'd run from the house last spring. "You wouldn't know the devil unless he snuck up from behind you an' drove his pitchfork straight up 'yer pert little ass."

Momma flipped the switch. The driveway floodlight snapped on, swamping the yard with a sick yellow glare. Both boys blinked up into the sudden light, their pupils fat black holes. Another cheap trick Momma might've said, meant to warn and scare like the bright bands on a coral snake, like the first few shots from an ill-used gun.

Noland fell back, stumbling over the stiff block of his brother's feet. It would've been funny, the tangled slump of his arms colliding with the tree stump knees of his brother except Momma pulled back hard on the trigger another time, a shot that caught the big boy in the belly. A damned unlucky go if there ever was one. The boy fell onto the flat of his back and coughed a little.

"Oh shit," Momma said.

Noland picked their Red Rider up from the ground, pushing through the scrub grass for his brother. Garrett must've had him by at least fifty pounds, but Noland hooked his brother by the arm pits and made to drag him away. Another thirty yards and they'd have Momma's gardening shed to shelter them, the lattice work of rotten wood and rusted tenpenny nails screening them at least well enough to cow Momma out've taking another wild shot. Maybe, for a second, that poor giant of a boy believed that he and his brother would both be leaving the old witch's yard alive.

"My momma doesn't know where we are," Garrett called, his hands sliding through the slick scraps of his shirt. "I don't mean to worry her so much."

Noland moved slow, but he turned for the closer cover and hauled his brother into the corn. It'd be a long trek home for the brothers. Wasn't nothing out that way but a defunct Valero still advertising its gas at a dollar twenty-nine and I doubted they would make it that far. We stood for a time, me and Momma, watching them go, the little one all out of smart things to say, the big one almost out of blood.

"Ain't nothing to be done for you now," Momma said, "an' I'm real sorry 'bout that."

Would've been better to lay the gun down, to pick up the set of spare truck keys hanging from the hook inside the door and head off to the Sea Horse, where Marshall would charge us double for half glasses of foam pored beer. But after a while, I stepped off Momma's porch, the dawn not but a few hours off, the Savage 110 in my own hands.

"Don't let them get too far," Momma said, heading in to bed.

Out in the fields, waves of corn dipped around a northern wind that came in from over the county line, bringing with it the promise of snow and the barbecue meat smell of an open fire. Harvest dry stalks rattled against each other, a skeletal sound like the rasp of locust wings. The whole history of the valley could be heard in that noise, a timeline of men struggling against the land and against each other. By then, I couldn't much tell if it was the boys rustling the tufts at the top of the stalks, or if it was just the wind.

BIOGRAPHIES

WILLOW ALVAREZ is a trans woman born and raised in Iowa. She's always liked fantasy and writing and recently graduated with a degree in English. She hopes to show the life of transwomen in her work, the good, the bad, and the ugly.

When not brewing up adult beverages, playing with strange soundmaking devices, or immersing herself in Patient Advocacy, the works of LEAH BOND have appeared in places such as Hinnom Magazine and Hobart Pulp. She is a staff writer for the fellows over at Legends of Tabletop, and resides with her husband in a peaceful suburb on the outskirts of Kansas City.

E.D. BURNETTE blames her reading of Stephen King's IT as a child for not outgrowing her fear of clowns and spiders. Her short fiction has appeared in *The Molotov Cocktail* and *The Weird and Whatnot*. She also writes not-so-scary stuff under her alter ego Danielle Burnette, who can be found at www.danielleburnette.com. She lives in northern California.

JANELLE M. EVANS is a woman of color, and the first in her family to attend college. She graduated summa cum laude from Arizona State University with a bachelor's degree in English and creative writing. She subsequently attended the University of Nevada Las Vegas (UNLV) and earned her Master of Fine Arts degree in Writing for Dramatic Media. She is an avid reader and writer of screenplays, novels, and short stories. She was thrilled to place in the top ten percent of 2015's Austin Film Festival, and the top five percent of the Oscar's Academy Nicholl Fellowship.

From the rainy Pacific Northwest, EMMA MACLEOD is a fiction writer and book adventurer, currently working on a double major for Creative Writing and Kinesiology. When she is not MIA at Powell's bookstore in Portland, Emma is usually found outside on a paddle board trying to soak in the little sun available. She is currently an unpublished writer.

MAX CARREY currently lives in sunny California, but will be moving to a gloomier location much like the settings in her stories (hopefully without the tragedy and mayhem involved). She's had stories appear in *Zimbell House's The Dead Game and Spirit Walker. Chipper Press' The Princess.* As well as upcoming releases with: *Temptation Press, PCC Inscape Magazine,* and *Impulsive Walrus.* To stay up to date follow her at: instagram.com/maxcarrey/

MICAELA MICHALK is an emerging writer from Canton, OH. She has a BA in psychology from Malone University where she also studied creative writing. Previous publications include *Pas De Deu* in *30N, The Hospital in Polaris, and Holding the Universe Together* in *The Scriblerus.*

DONNA J. W. MUNRO'S pieces are published in *Dark Moon Digest # 34, Flash Fiction Magazine, Astounding Outpost, Nothing's Sacred Magazine IV* and *V, Corvid Queen, Hazard Yet Forward* (2012), *Enter the Apocalypse* (2017), *Beautiful Lies, Painful Truths II* (2018), *Terror Politico* (2019), *Burning Love, Bleeding Hearts* (2020), *Borderlands 7* (2020), and others. Her upcoming novel, *Revelations: Poppet Cycle 1,* will be published by Omnium Gatherum in 2020. Contact her at https://www.donnajwmunro.com or @DonnaJWMunro on Twitter.

KACIE PROLOGO is a Rust Belt writer whose spent her life wrapped up in the kinds of familial mythology that runs rampant in her hometown of Alliance, Ohio. As a student in the Northeast Ohio Master of Fine Arts Creative Writing program, Kacie spends her time translating this family folklore into both fiction and nonfiction. Her work has been featured in *Scribble* magazine and *Fearsome Critters*.

SYLVIA SON lives in Mississauga and writes. She likes horror movies, improv and board games but not at the same time. But she has played Ultimate Werewolf and it sort of the same thing.

JAMILLA D. VANDYKE-BAILEY is a millennial black feminist living with mental illness and a dream. She uses her writing to give a voice to the trauma that is often suffered in silence and to bring a sense of belonging amongst the misfits. She has had work published in *The Southhampton Review, K'in Literary Journal,* and *Oddball Magazine*, amongst others.

www.ingramcontent.com/pod-product-compliance
Lightning Source LLC
Chambersburg PA
CBHW011442170626
46807CB00009B/3281